I0669309

Whisper When You Say My Name

Shonda Mayes

Grit, Grind, and Grace Publications

ISBN: 979-8-9860074-0-3

ISBN: 979-8-9860074-1-0

www.ShondaMayes.com

Cover by: Kreations K

First Edition

Prinited in the United States of America

This book is dedicated to my Grandmothers Ann Williams and Eunity Mayes. I pray that I have made you proud. Also to my daughters. I fight for my dreams so that you both know it can be done! I love you!

Trigger Warning

"My eyes once sparkled, but now they're dead. That's what happens when I listen to the voices in my head. I don't want them to see. I don't want them to know. Can't let my demons out to give them a show. I tried to fight. I wanted to win. But my demons were bigger than me in the end."

Prologue

I'll never forget the day my mama, Winter Carrington, found out my daddy was cheating on her. She locked herself in her bedroom, and all I heard for hours was her wailing from the pit of her soul. I tried to comfort her by wrapping my little arms around her, but she pushed me away. My love wasn't enough to help her. She needed something I wasn't capable of giving her.

Completely oblivious to my presence, she spent her time getting high, fucking, or crying. She gave me little to no attention for days at a time. Starving, I licked the remnants of the peanut butter and jelly that stained the dingy, white tank top I'd been wearing for the last week. It was from the sandwich I ate three days ago. That was the last time I had something to eat after one of her "friends" stopped by to bring her something to take the edge off and took pity on me.

Experience was a good teacher, so I tried to pick and choose when I asked my mother for anything. The last time I asked to go for something to drink, I received a back hand to the side of my face that left me dizzy. I tried hard to stay out of my mother's way because I feared what she might do to me next, but the way my stomach was touching my backbone, I could no longer take it.

"*Mama, I'm hungry,*" *I said with tears in my eyes. I stood ashamedly in the doorway of her bedroom, scared of what she might do to me.*

"*And you're telling me this for what? Here, have some heroin. It'll take away that hunger,*" *she said, shoving her stash of drugs in my tiny hands. I started crying, and it only angered her more.* "*Get your little nappy headed ass out of my face!*"

When she did pay any attention to me, it was to whip my ass because I reminded her of my father and all the pain he caused her. This went on for weeks, maybe even months. Hell, I don't even remember because I tried to suppress the pain that was inflicted upon me by my mother. The one who was supposed to love and nurture me wasn't capable. She lived in her own little world, and I was just an intruder that reminded her of the things she wanted to forget.

Even though she blamed me for my father's transgressions, it didn't change the way I felt about him. I loved my dad, and I knew he loved me. He never let the streets stop him from being in my life up until he got locked up. My grandmother took me to jail to see him one time, but he told her to never bring me back there again. He didn't want me to see him locked up in a cage. That didn't stop him from wanting to know about my grades and how I was maintaining given my circumstances.

My mother spent countless hours talking to the voices in her head. I am not quite sure when her mind fractured, but it was clear that at some point she'd lost her shit. One night I awoke to the sound of a strange voice. I thought it was one of Winter's friends who had come by. Getting out of my bed, I crept down the hallway to find my mother. My eyes bucked out of my little head when I saw no one there but her sitting on the side of the bed. Her eyes were wild, and her long hair looked like barbed wire set atop her head. What I heard next I would never forget. The sound of the strange voice coming from my mother's mouth caused my heart to nearly beat out of my chest. She looked like my mom, but the voice was not the one I was used to hearing come from her mouth. That image and that sound stayed with me.

It seemed she was entertained either by the voices in her head, which only got worse when she used drugs, or the men she brought around for money and drugs. Nowhere in between that was there any care or concern for my well being. At the time, there seemed to be no one who truly cared about me. My mother isolated us from our family, because I suspected that she was too ashamed of what her life had become. So, there wasn't anyone who knew what I was going through, but I always felt like there was someone or something in the shadows watching me.

So, I had to do what I had to do to survive with a drug addicted, mentally ill mother. Me surviving meant finding comfort within. I created worlds in my mind just to cope with the day to day. In my world, my parents were like Claire and Cliff Huxtable, and I had a bunch of siblings who adored and protected me. This was my strategy to make it through the day. Pretending I was somewhere and someone else. Watching my mother talk to herself, hallucinate, and get high was too much for me to bear.

After not hearing from my mother for a few months, my GiGi, who was my mother's mother, came looking for us. When she found me, I was hiding in a cabinet in the kitchen. Matted hair and dirty, too small clothes adorned my frail body. Winter was passed out on the bathroom floor with her dress over head and panties down to her ankles. She'd been on a drug binge.

"Winter! Winter! Get up! Lord, Jesus! Please don't let my baby girl be dead!" GiGi screamed. After GiGi called the ambulance, they showed up and gave Winter a dose of NarCan to bring her back Earth-side. Once the ambulance left with Winter in tow, GiGi spent the next hour praying and anointing the house with oil. She was casting out demons left and right. So much so that eventually I thought that when she casted some of them out they decided to latch on to me. Gigi was a woman of incredible faith. She believed that one day Winter would change and get herself together. I had little faith in her ability to change her ways. It was clear where her heart lied. She was more interested in maintaining a relationship with a man who didn't want her than being a mother to a little girl who didn't ask to be in this cruel world.

"Sugar baby, you ain't never got to worry about being hurt again. GiGi is gonna take good care of you," my grandmother said to me after she finished praying and anointing the house. I didn't have much to say. In fact, it took months before I would speak at all. GiGi thought I might be autistic, but doctors assured her that I wasn't. I just decided to suppress my voice, thinking that no one cared what I had to say or how I felt. The load I carried at five years old was heavy. Real heavy. But, that's when my new best friend showed up and helped me find my voice again.

"Don't be scared, Autumn," Kalidah said. "I'll always be here to help you. I'll never let anything bad happen to you and I'll always be by your side to protect you."

That was the beginning of a relationship I now wish I could be free from. A relationship that threatened to ruin the life I longed for. Kalidah was starting to become demanding, and she desperately wanted to take over my life

Present Day
Ezrail

A slight chill filled the air as the light wind whispered through the darkness of the night sky. I sat on the third-floor balcony of my apartment, taking in the scenes of the cityscape, yet keeping my eyes focused on my mark. I took a drag from the tightly rolled blunt that rested on my lips. A smirk covered my face as I watched her in the darkness.

She was a beauty to behold as she walked across the parking lot in deep conversation with a tall, caramel-complected man. Her long, dark curly hair blew in the wind, and it was evident she was very comfortable with him. He opened the door of his Mercedes Benz, and she hopped in. The man leaned in and kissed her before they pulled off.

I watched as the car trailed off into the night. I couldn't help but think of how much of an asset she would be to my team. She possessed a beauty that would make the strongest niggas weak at the sight of her. Yet, she still had an innocence that made her naïve enough to be molded into what I needed her to be. Plus, I knew there was a side of her she was trying to tuck away that needed to be released.

My thoughts were interrupted by bright white light emanating from the opening of the sliding glass door of my apartment. Alya came into view dressed in a white pantsuit. The light danced on the sequins covering the suit, making Alya look like she was glowing. I winced at the brightness of the light she brought with her.

"So you just popping up to a nigga's crib unannounced? What you doing around this side of town at this hour, Ma? This ain't usually your tour of duty," I questioned.

"I see you're keeping an eye on our girl," Alya responded while ignoring my questions.

"Of course. I'm waiting for the right moment to introduce myself to her and show her the plan. Where you goin all dressed up, Ma? Looking for new people to join your team?"

"I'm always looking for new people to join the team. That's what I'm destined to do. Don't worry about where I'm going. It's not like you'd join me there anyway. Now, back to our girl... What if she doesn't go for your plan? I may have a better offer for her."

"We'll see. You don't play dirty enough. She just needs to feel like she's accepted and ok to be her true self. She needs to see the value of what she thinks is a curse. I think my offer will be the one that suits her best. I'm just waiting for the right opportunity to introduce her to a whole new world."

"You've always been one to put your cart before the horse. I wouldn't bet on easily winning her over just yet. She's been through a lot. She wants something different. I'm not sure you can provide that. Sometimes a gentler approach is the right one."

"See, that's the thing with you. You always gotta be so soft and gentle. A girl like her doesn't respond to that type of shit."

"Ezrail, watch your mouth! You know I can't stand to hear people curse. You can communicate without the use of foul language. You've been given the gift of articulating yourself well. Try using it sometimes."

"My bad. What I'm saying is this, though. When you come into the room, you aren't loud enough. She'll hear you, but eventually, she'll realize my voice is the loudest in the room. She'll have no choice but to hear me, and I'll make her an offer she can't refuse."

"An offer she can't refuse, huh? Your so-called offers have expiration dates and usually leave your team members in worse shape than when you found them. You'd think after all this time, you'd be tired of this."

"It's the way it is sometimes, but I never lose. My team might take a hit, but I never lose. I always complete my mission."

"Just know this, pride always comes before a fall. By the looks of things, you're way overdue," Alya said as she turned and disappeared just as fast as she arrived.

Chapter One
Autumn

I sat on top of my fiance, Lucky Santiago, winding my waist and gripping his penis with my slippery, wet vagina. He gripped my waist to find my rhythm. He was getting close to his release, and I wasn't ready for him to cum just yet. I hopped off abruptly, ruining his intention to splatter his seeds into my pussy this time. Not that I didn't welcome the idea of having his baby, but at this moment I was focused on fulfilling his sexual appetite, so I didn't have to worry about him giving my dick to another bitch.

"Baby, what you doing?" Lucky asked. I didn't say a word. I slid down on the bed to finish what we started. Hungrily, I took his dick in my mouth and began slurping my juices from it with intensity.

"Shit!" I heard Lucky moan as I spat on his dick, took it in my mouth again, and tightened my grip as I sucked it. I could taste the saltiness of his pre-cum oozing into my mouth.

"What's my name, baby? I need you to say it, but not too loud!"

"Autumn, baby! Autumn, I love when you suck the shit out of my dick." Hearing him say my name and tell me that he liked the way I was serving him made my already wet pussy drip even more. So, I went crazy on his dick and sucked him until he climaxed in my mouth, swallowing every drop of his cum like he liked.

"That shit was amazing!"

"I know." I eased off the bed and went into the bathroom to get a warm towel to clean him up. After wiping my man down, I went into the bathroom to take a shower. When I finished cleaning myself up, I returned to the bedroom to find my Lucky in a deep sleep. I joined him in the bed and watched him while he slept.

Lucky was everything I wanted. He had street nigga edge just like my father but had given up the streets to get money legally. Lucky used the money he made from the drug game to purchase his barbershop and a couple of properties that he rented out on Section Eight. He wasn't dope boy paid anymore, but he was doing well for himself since leaving the game. The fact that he reminded me of my father as well as his business acumen were just two of the reasons I fell so hard for him.

He fit into my dream of having my version of the perfect family. My vision is for us to be a power couple and dominate in our respective fields. My dream was to finish school as a registered nurse and eventually open an agency that provided freelance opportunities to nurses.

Time was of the essence. I wasn't getting any younger and had already invested two years of my life into being his woman.

Although we were engaged, we had yet to set a date and walk down the aisle. It was no way in hell I was going to be one of those women who would be a forever fiancé. At some point, he was going to meet me at the altar. He owed that to me.

There was nothing more that I wanted than to be a wife and a mother. Thoughts of hearing tiny little footsteps running around this apartment invaded my mind constantly. The only problems were that Lucky didn't want kids yet, and we weren't married. I was determined to break the family curse of having kids out of wedlock

"You know why he doesn't want to marry you or have any babies with you with your crazy ass! Stop playing yourself! I'm only trying to make sure you don't get hurt."

"Shut up! Damn!" I said aloud.

"Babe, who you talking to and why you talking like that?" Lucky asked, rolling over to face me. He looked perplexed, and I'm sure I looked like a deer in headlights

"Oh, uhhh, nobody. I want to talk to you about something, though." I rested my head on the back of the headboard and pulled the comforter up to my chin.

"What, babe? Can't it wait? I'm trying to sleep." He rolled back over, turning his back toward me. This was typical of him. It seemed like he never wanted to talk about any of the things that concerned me.

"Where do you see our relationship going? We've been together for two years, engaged for six months now, and I'm ready to start a family."

"Babe, don't start this shit right now. You know all the shit I got going on!"

"And I've been holding you down through all the shit you

got going on. Shit, if that don't make me wife worthy, I don't know what will."

"Autumn, pressing a nigga ain't gonna make me set a wedding date or pump no babies in you any faster! This shit is getting exhausting. Let's just go with the flow."

"Go with the flow? Go with the fucking flow? I been going with the flow and trying to believe that you're going to marry me. You asked me to marry you six months ago after I worried the hell out of you. It shouldn't take this long to know that you want to marry me and have a family with me by now. Lucky, we ain't getting any younger. I'm twenty-nine, and you're thirty-four. We're beyond the point of going with the flow. If we wait any longer, then my eggs gonna be too damn rotten to have a child. We need to get married soon. Knowing you, it's another reason you ain't trying to go ahead and take that trip down the aisle. So, which one of your hoes is it this time? Is it Traci? Or Renisha? Or is it Whitney this time?"

"See, this that bullshit that makes me question why I even asked you to marry me to begin with. No nigga want to come home to a nagging ass girl every day let alone a nagging ass wife! I didn't sign up for this bullshit. You too worried about getting married and having kids when what you need to do is clean this damn house and cook a nigga a meal. Look around this fucking room! All these damn clothes on the floor. Shit all over the dressers. Don't even let me get started on that filthy ass kitchen. I got you set up in a luxury apartment in Buckhead, yet you want to live like you're still in the fucking hood! All you want to do is nag the fuck out of me about having kids and cheating on your ass and spend up the money I give you for bills and shit on designer bags and clothes! Your priorities ain't in check enough to be worried about being a wife and some damn kids."

"Fuck you, nigga!!"

"Aye yo! You need to watch talking to me like that!" Lucky got up out of the bed, slid on a pair of gray sweat pants, and a white t-shirt. "Matter of fact, fuck this shit! I'm out! I'll be back when you get your mind right."

"Baby, wait! I'm sorry! It's just that I love you so much and I really want to be your wife. I want to start our little family. I won't say shit else about this right now. Get back in the bed." When Lucky didn't move, I got out of bed and tried to block our bedroom door. He would for sure go find comfort in another bitch's arms, and I didn't want that. All I really wanted was for him to see that I was all he needed. Not just his main chick, but the one and only woman he needed in his life.

"Look, Autumn, I hear you, but at this point, I need to clear my head. And, Imma give you time to think about some things. Think about whether or not losing me is gonna be worth all the nagging and bullshit you keep putting me through day in and day out. I already told you I got enough shit on my plate without you adding unnecessary drama to it."

"Aight, baby. I'm sorry. I'm gonna chill. I promise you that."

"Nah, don't keep apologizing. I told you the best apology you could ever give me is changed behavior." With that, Lucky walked out the door. Like a little flunky for him, I ran to the window and watched him as he got in his Benz and pulled off.

As anger welled up inside me, I grabbed a picture frame containing a photo of me and Lucky from my coffee table and hurled it at the wall next to the front door. It hit the ground, shattering into pieces and leaving even more of a mess for me to clean up in my filthy apartment.

I sat down on my couch feeling defeated. I hated when I couldn't control my anger at times. Sometimes, I felt like I was turning into my mother, which was a scary thought. As beautiful as my mother was, she could turn downright hideous when the voices took over her mind. For that reason, she spent much of my life and hers on drugs and in and out of mental health facilities. The last thing I wanted was to become any resemblance of the woman she was, even though I loved her.

I settled on the couch and decided to watch reruns of *Living Single* with the hope that the sandman would visit me. Deep down, I wanted to believe Lucky would come back home, but I knew better. When Lucky got mad at me and left the house, it usually meant I wouldn't see him for the rest of the night. I'd be lucky if he came back home tomorrow morning.

I woke up the next morning feeling groggy. I mostly slept with one eye open in case Lucky decided he wanted to bring his ass home. He didn't though, so I knew I had to do whatever it took to make things right between us.

I looked around our apartment and decided to clean up. Having a beautiful, luxury apartment in Buckhead wasn't shit if it was dirty. Neither was living like trash, and there was no way I could be the perfect wife or have the perfect family living like this.

Even though the apartment was in my name, Lucky took care of most of the bills, including the rent. He didn't want me to have to worry about bills while I pursued my nursing degree. So, I definitely could do better at showing my appreciation by cleaning this nasty ass apartment up. Besides, he was right. Who wants a wife who keeps a nasty ass home?

I started in the kitchen because it needed the most work. I washed the dishes that had been piled up and crusted with food for the last week, emptied the dishwasher, mopped, and cleaned every surface from top to bottom. The gray and white marble countertops sparkled once I was done wiping them down.

Before I hit the rest of the house. I decided to Instacart some groceries so I could cook Lucky's favorite meal. He loved when I made my famous chicken alfredo, breadsticks, and salad. I completed my order and moved on to tidy up the living room, did our laundry, cleaned the bathrooms, and our room.

Once I finished, I looked around my apartment, proud of myself for the job I'd done. Cleaning took up most of the day. It was never that I was bad at cleaning. When I got home from work, I never felt like cleaning, so sometimes I let shit get out of control before I decided to clean up. Lucky hated it, though.

My Instacart order came just in time. I quickly prepared the meal and called Lucky. He didn't answer, though. I decided to snap a pic of the meal I'd prepared hoping it would entice him into coming home. It didn't. He didn't respond to any of the messages I sent.

Pissed, I decided to ride out to see if I could pinpoint where Lucky was. I threw on my gray Pink sweatsuit and a pair of

Airmaxes to match. I wanted to be comfortable in case I rolled up on something that would cause me to have to throw hands. I jumped in my 745i and decided to take the twenty-minute ride to Lucky's Barbershop in Decatur.

Part of the reason he pressed me so much about getting back in school and finishing my nursing degree was so that we could get into the adult group and nursing home industry as well as concierge nursing services. Lucky viewed it as another opportunity for us to add another lucrative stream of income.

I pulled up to the barbershop. I didn't see Lucky's car, but that didn't stop me from going in to find out where the fuck he was. The shop was jumping. It seemed like every nigga on the block was in there to get a cut. Eyes of almost every man in there roamed my body as I walked past them to get to the back. That was usually how it went when I entered a room, though. My pretty milk chocolate brown skin, long hair, wide hips, and phat ass always turned heads. I lacked nothing in the beauty area, and I was all-natural cornbread and collard greens thick.

"What's up, Joe? You seen Lucky?" I asked. Joe was standing behind his chair lining up a customer. He looked up at me licking ashy ass lips. Joe was far from being anywhere near attractive, so him standing there gawking at me instead of answering my question made me feel even more sick to my stomach than I already felt.

"Nah. I ain't seen him. What you need, though? You know I got you," Joe said as he adjusted his dick with his hand. "You need some of this?" The other niggas in earshot laughed but I didn't find a thing funny. Niggas always wanted to be cute when Lucky or or his boy and shop manager, June wasn't around.

"Nigga, keep being slick. You know Lucky don't like that shit and you ain't got a motherfucking thing I want other than for you to tell me where my man is at," I replied.

"I said I ain't seen the nigga since earlier, and I ain't keeping track of another nigga. Besides, if he wanted you to know where he was at, he would have told your dumb ass," Joe spat.

"Nigga fuck you! And put some Vaseline on them crusty ass lips. All the licking in the world ain't gonna do shit to help the baboon's ass you call your mouth!" Laughter erupted as an evil look emerged on Joe's face. That's what his ass got, though. He loved running his mouth. I'm sure he wanted to say something else but thought better of it. I stormed out of the shop and hopped in my car mad as hell.

"Girl, you already know where that nigga at. You know he probably got some hoe sliding up and down his dick right now. I don't know why you put yourself through this."

I decided there was no point in me continuing to ride around looking for Lucky and looking stupid. I called my friend Tamela.

"Hey, girl, what you doing?"

"Nothing. Why what's up?" Tam asked.

"I wanted to see if you wanted to go to Hudson Grille to get something to eat and grab a drink."

"Yeah, girl. I ain't doing nothing else. You want me to pick you up or do you wanna to meet there?"

"I'm already out, so just meet me over there. How long is it gonna take you to get ready?"

"Give me a good forty-five minutes and I'll be there."

I hung up the phone and decided to try and calling Lucky

again, but of course this nigga wasn't answering his phone. The thought of riding by that bitch, Whitney's house briefly entered my mind, but it would have taken entirely too long for me to head to Gwinnett County to scope out her house and be back in time to meet Tamela.

I pulled up to Hudson Grille and went inside to get me and Tam a table. The waiter approached me and took my drink order. Just as the waitress was bringing me my drink, Tamela called me.

"Sis, where you at?" I asked.

"I'm coming in now. Where you sitting at?"

"Come towards the back. You'll see me."

"You want me to come back?" My waiter, Danny asked.

"Yeah, give us about five minutes and can you bring my friend a Grey Goose and cranberry?"

"I got you," Danny said and walked off.

"What's up, girl?" Tamela greeted. I stood up to give her a hug. It didn't matter where Tam went, she was going to make sure she was dressed to impress. She looked amazing in her jeans, Fendi sweater, and matching Fendi boots. Her long honey blonde tresses were pulled up in a messy bun and complimented her honey brown, heart-shaped face. Tam was a certified head turner just like me. That's why we clicked so well.

"Girl, same shit just a different day."

"Let me guess. Lucky still got your ass stressing? I don't know why you continue to put up with his shit. How long is it gonna take you to realize that nigga don't love nothing but the streets and getting his dick wet?"

"So you just gone sit down and start going in on me about Lucky. You know I love him. I done gave that nigga two years, and I be damned if I'm gonna let another bitch come in and take what's mine."

"A bitch can't fuck up what you got anyway. Only Lucky can do that. Last time I checked, that nigga belonged to the streets. You might want to consider giving him back and save yourself some heartache and pain while you can."

"You're right. I know he's cheating, but what nigga you know gonna admit to that? Everytime I bring up where our relationship is going, he flips that shit back on me. He probably off with some bitch as we speak. He didn't come home last night."

"Girl, there's a quick fix for that. All you gotta do is get a tracker and put it on his car in a spot he will never check. That way, you can find out what you need to know and that nigga won't be able to deny it."

"Bitch, let me find out you be on some *Inspector Gadget* shit!"

"And do! One thing I ain't about is getting played, so you know I gotta stay ten steps ahead of the game at all times." We both laughed. Tamela never got too comfortable with a man. As soon as they flipped the script on her, she did the same and let their asses go. Her motto was that men come a dime a dozen and given that she was the prize, she wasn't putting up with any bullshit. I felt her, but this shit I have with Lucky is different.

"I'm going to send you the link to the tracker I normally use. It's cheap and you can link it to your phone."

"I didn't ask for you to send me no damn link!"

"I know. But I also know you, so in order to prevent you from asking later, I already sent them damn links. Anyway, let's change the subject. What's up with you going back to school? I just finished my registration. Did you finish yours?"

"Nah, I still owe about three stacks before I can register. I gotta figure out a way to get that money so I can go back. I don't want to keep lying to everybody about me being in school."

"So, you mean to tell me your man has one of the most successful barbershops in Atlanta, you wear just about designer everything, but you ain't got three stacks to register for your classes? What part of the game is that?" Tam asked.

"Girl, I can't ask Lucky for the money. He gave it to me already. I took that money and spent it on that MJB Louis bag I wanted. He been getting on me about how I spend my money."

"You need to get your shit together. I'm only telling you this because I'm your friend. You're too busy focused on keeping Lucky and you're not prioritizing your dreams. You always talking about you want you and Lucky to be a power couple, but that shit ain't gonna happen if you keep up this shit. Can't you pick up some extra shifts or something at work?"

"Okay, mama," I sarcastically replied. "And when am I gonna have time to spend with my man? Plus, you already know I don't make enough money as a Nursing Assistant to get that kind of cash up in a short amount of time. I'm going to figure something out, though."

"Whatever, Autumn," Tam responded.

I dropped the conversation about Lucky and school. Instead of continuing to harp on my problems, we talked about planning our next girls' trip and Tamela's new boo thang. Spending time with my best friend was a welcome distraction and prevented me from driving around town looking for a nigga that clearly didn't want to be found.

We wrapped up our night and I headed home to spend another sleepless night alone, wondering where the nigga I loved was laying his head.

Chapter Two
Autumn

I pulled up to work, dreading having to clock in for my shift. As much as I wanted to be a nurse, I despised having to do the menial tasks that being a Nursing Assistant entailed – like wiping shit from the backside of a wrinkled-up ass – but I had to do what I had to do. Even though Lucky was once known in the streets for getting money and now having a successful barbershop, I didn't want to have to depend on his money alone. I dreamed of being my own boss, and me sitting on my ass every day wasn't gonna make that happen.

I got out of my car and reluctantly walked into Mr. Theodore Kessler's apartment at the facility I worked at. He was a rich old white man who was now the responsibility of his affluent daughter who did not have the time to care for him. So, she left that up to people like me and the other nurses and home health aides that shuffled through the facility throughout the day and night.

"Hey, Autumn. How you?" Ms. Angelique asked as I entered the front door. Her plump, brown cheeks rose into a smile showcasing the one gold tooth she had on the left side of her mouth. She was a sweet older lady who took me under her wing when I started here. She was like another mother figure to me.

"Hey, Ms. Angie. I'm alright. I ain't feel like coming in here. I've been super tired lately, but you know how that go."

"I feel you, baby. I left you a plate of ribs, greens, and mac and cheese in the refrigerator for your lunch," Ms. Angie said. She loved bringing me plates of her home-cooked meals. I enjoyed her bringing them just as much as she enjoyed bringing them to me. "I already prepped Mr. Kessler's food, so he should be good for a while. This shift shouldn't be so bad. He's resting. You know he had a procedure a few days ago, so the meds keep him knocked out for most of the day."

"Ok, Thank you! I don't mean any harm, but I'm glad his old behind will be knocked out. I need to make some calls about my entry into nursing school."

"You better get that straight! I know your granny will be so proud when you graduate from that school as a registered nurse. I'm proud of you, too baby."

"Aww, thank you Ms. Angie. I appreciate that."

"Well let me get on outta here so I can get on home. My daughter is picking me up to go see my grandbaby in her school program, and I don't want to have them waiting on me."

"Alright. Have a good morning. I will see you tomorrow."

Ms. Angelique left, and I went in to check on Mr. Kessler. When I got to his bedroom door, the scent of shit permeated the air. The smell filled my nostrils, causing my stomach to turn as I tried to control the contents of my stomach from rising up in my throat and spilling onto the floor. My stomach had already been queasy for the last few days, and this wasn't helping me none.

"Damn! I don't feel like doing this bullshit! Ms. Angie knew this dude took a shit before she left," I mumbled under my breath. Ms. Angie would always get me like that. She hated cleaning Mr. Kessler's shitty ass just like I did, and if he decided to blow every piece of food he ate out his ass before her shift ended, she wasn't changing him. So, that left me to deal with the shit. Literally.

"Hey there. Come on in here and give me some sugar. You sure are pretty for a colored," Mr. Kessler said. I thought this geezer was asleep, yet here he was laying up in a pile of his feces, calling me a colored, and flirting. At nearly ninety years old, he was stuck in a time that didn't exist anymore. I ignored him and cleaned his saggy ass up so I could get to the things on my personal to-do list.

After leaving Mr. Kessler in his room to continue resting, I pulled out my phone to call the nursing school I was trying to get into to see what the hold up was with my paperwork. I stayed on the phone for a whole forty-five minutes just for them to tell me that I couldn't enroll until I paid the three thousand dollar balance I owed.

Disappointed was an understatement for how I felt. I only had one more year left before I would be able to finish school, and a measly three thousand dollars was gonna be the thing that stopped me. All my life I dreamed of being a nurse. I genuinely loved taking care of other people. Some days this job really worked my nerves, but there was a sense of joy that I felt when given the opportunity to help make another person feel good. That was, of course, without having to clean shit off their ass.

I went back in the house to check on Mr. Kessler. He was sound asleep, but his vitals needed to be checked again. I decided to let him rest and check them later. Instead, I really needed to talk to Lucky. I dialed his number.

"Where the fuck you been, Lucky? What bitch you decided to stay with last night?"

"So this what you want to do? A nigga leaves the house because you on some bullshit, and this is how you want to start the conversation? You always bringing negativity to me. Damn!"

"Babe, I'm sorry, but what else am I supposed to think when you don't come home?"

"Hmmm. I don't know. Maybe that a nigga was just trying to clear his head because his girl stay stressing him."

"Whatever. Ok, I don't even want to keep arguing anymore. There's plenty of food left from last night if you plan on going back to the house. I gotta get back in here and check on Mr. Kessler."

"Autumn, look. You know I love you, but you need to chill the fuck out sometimes. I know you want to get married and all that, but a nigga like me gotta lot of shit to take care of in these streets before I can settle down and start a family."

"I hear you. I'll see you when I get off." I returned back to Mr. Kessler's room. He was awake but lying there quietly. I was thankful because when he started talking sometimes, he didn't know what to say out of his mouth. It took all of me not to rock him in his shit from time to time.

I went into Mr. Kessler's closet to retrieve some clean chucks to line his bed with. I was sure he'd soiled the last one while he was sleeping. A small brown wooden box partially blocked my entrance into the closet. Of course it piqued my curiosity. I went to pick it up, but it slipped out of my hands, hitting the floor, spilling the contents.

My eyes bulged and damn near hit the floor at the sight of the contents of the box. I bent down to retrieve the stacks of money that lay splattered on the floor. As I placed each band of hundred-dollar bills back into the box, I counted thirty grand.

"Just go ahead and take the money. He ain't gonna miss it."

"What you in there doing, gal?" Mr. Kessler asked, startling me. It took all of me not to take this money or at least as much of it as I could conceal, but I didn't. I put the box back in the corner and proceeded to handle my business.

Before my shift ended, I headed to the kitchen to grab the food Ms. Angie left for me. My mouth watered at the thought of enjoying Ms. Angie's food. My feet were throbbing from spending so much time on them, but at the end of the day, the experience on this job would help me further my career goal.

My phone rang, and I looked down to see my grandmother, Roberta Carrington's, name on my iPhone screen. I answered it as quickly as possible. Other than Lucky, she's the only person I drop everything for.

"Hey, GiGi! How are you?" I answered excitedly.

"Hey, my Sugar Baby! I'm alright. When you coming by the house? I need to talk to you about something."

"Probably in a couple days. What's wrong? You need something?"

"Well, Sugar Baby, I didn't want to tell you this over the

phone, but I just found out I got breast cancer. Stage two breast cancer."

"What? Are you sure, GiGi?" Tears welled up in my eyes at the thought of losing my grandmother. She was all I had and the only consistent person in my life. Losing her would mean I would be losing a big part of me, and there is no way I could handle that right now.

"Yes, Sugar, but I'm gonna be just fine. Don't you go sitting around worrying about me. I got Jehovah Rapha, my God who heals, on my side and I'm standing on His word. I'm already healed by his stripes."

"I hear you, GiGi," I said. One thing about it, GiGi was gonna give God all the credit. She was serious about her faith and her relationship with God. I, on the other hand, wavered most of the time. I only wished I had the capacity to believe in God the way GiGi did. It was so many nights I begged God to help my mama get off drugs and to bring my daddy home from jail, but I was certain He didn't hear my cries.

"Do you have to have any surgeries? Radiation or Chemo?" I asked.

"Yes, I gotta get this lump removed. Then, after that, I start my Chemo. My procedure is in a few days. I just don't know how I am going to keep my bills around here paid and afford all the medicine I need. Medicare don't cover everything. I guess I'll just have to keep standing on the promises of God. He ain't never failed me yet!"

"Well, how much you need, GiGi? I don't want you worrying about no bills and meds. I'll see what I can do to help you."

"Nah, baby. I don't want you taking on my stuff. I know

how you can make rash decisions sometimes. I don't want you choosing to do anything that's gonna get you in no trouble again. Don't worry about me."

"I do work, GiGi. I'm not out here stealing or doing any of the things I used to do. And you know I'm always going to worry about you. You're all I got."

"You know your mama is home now. She's staying with your Aunt Tweety until she can get up on her feet. She and Tweety gonna be there when I have my procedure. You know your mama can't wait to see you, so maybe you can come by here this week to see her. She's been here almost every day."

"Well, GiGi, no disrespect, but if Winter wanted to see me, why hasn't she called me? And I hope she's still on her meds." I couldn't bring myself to refer to the woman who birthed me as "Mom." GiGi was more of a mother to me than she had ever been.

"Winter will always be your mom, so you need to show some respect and stop calling her by her first name. I just pray that one day the two of you can have a good relationship. You gotta let the good Lord work on that heart of yours and forgive your mama. She's had a lotta crosses to bear and her life ain't been easy. Just hope you never have to go through the things she's been through. Winter is a good girl. She just made bad decisions that caused her to spiral out of control. I know you don't know this, but I wasn't always the best mother to Winter. I had my vices, too. Before I gave my life to the Lord, I had a serious problem with liquor. Your mama and your Aunt Tweety would sometimes find me face down in a plate of food or passed out on the bathroom floor. At the time, I was dating a man that would get me liquored up, just so he could try to have his way with your mother and your Aunt. I'd be so drunk that I didn't know what was going on. So, you see, Winter has a lot of baggage, too, and a lot of it is my fault. But my baby gave me grace. I prayed and prayed that one day she would forgive me, and she did. That's why I want you to forgive her. She deserves a little grace."

"I get it, GiGi. I really do. Maybe one day I can bring myself to forgive her. It's just a lot for me to take in. All that she did just don't sit well with me, GiGi. But for you, I'll come by. Please keep me posted about your appointments. I want to be there as much as I can."

"I will, baby. You take care of yourself and don't take too long before you decide to come by here. I love you."

"Ok, GiGi. I love you, too, and I'll see you soon." After I hung up with GiGi, I gathered my stuff to leave.

I appreciated everything my grandmother did to raise me. Things were hard for me, but GiGi tried her best to give me a decent life. When she could, she'd take me to get my nails painted and my hair done at the beauty salon she went to. Whatever she could do to bring a smile to my face, she tried to do. Even though GiGi didn't have much, she made sure I had the things I needed. When she learned I was struggling mentally and emotionally, she did everything she could to make sure I was ok. I always felt like she looked at me like a second chance because of how things turned out with my mother.

I pulled up to my apartment to see that Lucky hadn't made it in yet. Since it was clear he was still gonna take his time to bring his yellow ass home, I decided to take a hot shower and put something cute on for him. I figured I'd try to play nice and be sweet since I'd fucked up over the last couple of days. I didn't want to continue to be so negative about our relationship. Lucky was the one for me. That was it. Plain and simple.

After I finished taking my shower, I entered the living room to find Lucky sitting on the couch with a glass of henny and coke in his hand. He looked so fine sitting there with his button up on and a crisp pair of jeans. His thick, curly jet-black hair framed his face perfectly. He looked up at me with those beautiful, mesmerizing green eyes, and I instantly wanted to pull his dick out and sit on it.

I leaned in to kiss him. He quickly pecked me on the lips before getting up from his place on the couch. The coldness in his response told me he still wasn't fucking with me like that. The thing about Lucky was that he could hold a grudge like no other. Usually, it took him a couple of days before he warmed up to me again, so I wasn't surprised by his reaction. I was still going to try to smooth things over with him, though.

"Babe, you want me to fix you a plate?" I inquired. I really wanted the tension between us to be gone already.

"Yeah," he coldly responded. I headed in the kitchen anyway to fix his plate. I didn't know what to do to repair our relationship, but I wasn't a quitter. I just had to learn to always stop expecting the worst from him. Until I knew for a fact that he was cheating, I wouldn't say another word about it. In fact, I had been thinking lately if cheating was even a deal-breaker for me. All men cheated. Even the ugly ones. Lucky was fine and a well-known street nigga with money. There was no doubt in my mind that bitches were throwing pussy at him left and right. He'd cheated on me in the past. At least I suspected he had with a female hairstylist that used to work in his shop. I just didn't have concrete evidence that he did. I just thought I would be willing to accept his cheating versus losing my mind over him cheating like my mom did when she found out about the five other women my dad was fucking with at the same time she was carrying me.

"HE'S CHEATING. YOU KNOW DAMN WELL HE'S WITH SOME bitch. You called his phone five times today, and he didn't answer your call not one time. You know what time it is."

Things still weren't right with Lucky and I. I suffered through eating dinner with him in silence. We went to bed with our backs turned to each other. No kissing, no hugging, and definitely no sex. I hated going to bed mad. Not to mention I heard his cellphone vibrating inside the drawer of his nightstand all night long. Whoever was on that phone is probably the reason he's late coming home.

With rage brewing in my heart, I watched as Lucky pulled into a parking space in front of the building. He was oblivious to me sitting there and to the tongue lashing he was about to face although he should be used to it by now.

As soon as I saw him hop out of his car and head up the steps, I got up and headed to the front door to meet him. I snatched the door open and stood there with my arms folded across my chest.

"What took you so long this time?" I asked.

"I had to take June home. Didn't you get my text?" Lucky responded with a bewildered look that spread across his face. "Now move out my way."

"You a fucking lie! What text you talking about? I ain't get

34

no text! What bitch was it this time?" Lucky brushed passed me knocking me into the doorframe.

"Autumn, don't start with that bullshit again! I don't have time for this," Lucky said. "Didn't I just leave the fucking house the other night because you don't know how to keep your fucking mouth closed and let a nigga have some peace?"

"Fuck your peace! I don't get no peace when you out in them streets every other night with some bitch!"

"Aye yo! Watch your fucking mouth talking to me like that!" Lucky yelled, walking up on me. "That's your problem! You always worried about another female instead of worrying about what's going on in our house. You always gotta assume the worst. How many times I gotta tell you that if you keep thinking negative all the time, negative shit gone happen? You always have something negative to say. Why can't you just believe what I tell you?" Lucky headed into the kitchen to fix himself a drink. His caramel skin was flushed with a red tint that showed his anger brewing.

I knew how much he hated when I was on my bullshit. I couldn't help it though, my spidey senses told me he was lying. And I had a feeling I knew exactly who the bitch was that he had been keeping time with.

"Well, what other reason would you have for not coming home?" I asked. I was relentless in my belief that Lucky was cheating. I couldn't help it. In my mind, all men cheated. My father did it to my mother, and it caused her ass to go crazy. I wasn't too far behind her.

"Didn't I just tell you? I had to take June home. He hit me up after I left the barbershop and asked me if I could give him a ride home. His car is still down. I ain't got no reason to lie to you. Baby, you gotta chill. It's just me and you until it ain't. I'm not a cheater and if I ever feel like Imma cheat, I'll leave you first." Lucky walked over to me, pulled me close, and kissed my lips. For now, I would let this situation rock until I felt I couldn't anymore.

"Yo, you gotta get that shit under control. I don't know how much more of the false accusations I can take. I ain't gave you no reason to keep coming at me like this. You gotta chill the fuck out, shawty. For real!"

"You're right," I said as I got up from the table and headed to the bathroom. I needed a minute to clear my head. My anxiety was high, so I turned the water on and splashed my face.

I heard what Lucky said, but his actions told me otherwise. All this coming home late or not at all didn't sit well with my spirit. In my heart, I knew the time was coming when my worst fears would come true, and I didn't know how I would handle it all.

"That's what you have me for. I'll always protect you, but you won't let me."

I shook my head trying to erase the whisper of the voice I was hearing. It was getting louder by the day and that scared me. The last thing I wanted was for anyone close to me to know that I was hearing things.

I returned to the living room to find Lucky sitting on the couch on his phone. As soon as he heard me enter the room, he ended the call abruptly. I chose not to even address it. It was like beating a dead horse with him anyway.

Chapter Three
Autumn

The moonlight glistened from the night sky as I sat on my balcony with my thoughts. Sleep evaded me as I sipped on some ginger ale, trying to calm my nauseous stomach. There was so much on my mind from getting the money I needed for school, helping GiGi, to my relationship with Lucky. The truth was that no matter how I tried to convince myself that I would be okay with sharing Lucky with other women, I knew that was a lie.

I wanted him to myself for a lifetime. I wanted the big house in Sugar Hill or Suwanee, a son that looked just like his daddy, a little girl that looked like me, and a dog. Everything I never had as a child I wanted to give to my kids. I didn't want to lose my chance at a happy life due to another woman stealing his heart.

Fear kept me bound in so many ways. I was afraid that Lucky would find out my secret and I would lose him because of it. When I suspected he was cheating on me, it took a toll on my self-esteem. The voice in my head started as a whisper but were getting louder and trying to convince me to leave Lucky. I wouldn't, though. He'd have to leave me first. I was determined to make it work. There was no other man I wanted to be with, but the voice in my head always wanted to avenge me of any pain I suffered.

There was nothing I wanted more than to be the total opposite of my mom, but it seemed like the same demons that haunted her were here to claim me. I wasn't sure how long it would be before I could no longer run from them or her. Because it seemed like history was repeating itself with me, I was ashamed. I didn't want the stigma of being crazy attached to me.

"I'm not anything you should be ashamed of. One day you'll see."

Ignoring my demons, I stared out into the darkness as the crisp fall breeze kissed my face. A car crept by and pulled into a parking space close to my building. A man dressed in a black trench coat with a pair of Ray Bans adorning his face got out of the car. Why the hell he had sunglasses on when it was dark out was beyond me. It was my first time seeing him, so I figured he may be here to visit someone who lived in my building. He glanced in my direction and nodded his head. I waved, but his gaze penetrated my soul and made me uncomfortable. That shit made me so uncomfortable that I took my ass back in the house.

I eased back in my bed. Lucky was sleeping peacefully. He rolled over, opening his eyes and pulling me into him. It felt good to have his arms wrapped around me.

"Where you been at? Out on the patio again?" he asked.

"Yeah, I couldn't sleep. You know I love looking at the stars when I'm trying to get my mind right."

"Well, you better get your ass back in this bed and try to go to sleep."

"Maybe you can put me to sleep." I mounted Lucky and tried to pull his manhood from his boxers. He abruptly grabbed my arms and pushed me back to my side of the bed.

"Nah, I'm good on all that tonight."

"Oh really. So, now we not having sex?"

"I'm just tired. Don't make this shit turn into something that it's not. I don't feel like being on a seesaw with your crazy ass."

"First of all, don't call me crazy! I don't like that shit! Secondly, let me check your balls. If they still heavy, then at least I'll know you haven't emptied them out in some pussy that ain't mine."

"Bitch, have you lost your mind? This shit you talking is crazy! You ain't checking shit. Lay your ass down. I told you I'm just tired as shit."

"Whatever," I relented. I slid under my comforter and tried to get some sleep, but doubted I would. This was the first time Lucky ever turned down my pussy. I don't care what we went through, he was always down to slide inside my tight, wet pussy. That only meant one thing.

I GOT A LATE START TO MY DAY, WHICH IN TURN, CAUSED me to be late for work. The last thing I needed was for my supervisor, Georgette to be on my ass. She loved to find a reason to get in my shit. I knew she couldn't stand me. The feeling was definitely mutual, but I needed this job.

Given my current situation, I needed more money and to pick up more hours on this job. I didn't want to have to go to Lucky to ask him for anything else. I just had to have that MJB Louis bag. My irrational decisions had me back at square one with no one to blame but myself. Now I had to figure out how I was going to get that money.

I spent most of the morning washing Mr. Kessler's clothes and tidying up his room. I emptied his bed pan, changed his sheets, and gave him a sponge bath. I despised having to wipe the nasty old man down, but he enjoyed it. He had no problem letting me know that amongst other things I didn't care to know about him.

"Gal, when I was a youngin' I used to get all the Black poontang I wanted," Mr. Kessler said as I finished up his sponge bath.

"Is that right?" I replied. Clearly, Mr. Kessler was with the shits again today.

"Whatchu mean, 'Is that right?' Gal, you damn skippy I did! I coulda had yours, too!" I was amused. I couldn't imagine any woman giving him anything judging by the way he looked and how gross he talked all the time. The years hadn't been kind to him, and he was a weird looking man even in his younger years with a nose that made him look like Gonzo with beady, green eyes. But the thing he did have is money, and it was enough to buy him all the "poontang" he wanted. Just not mine, even though he offered money to me on multiple occasions.

After getting Mr. Kessler settled, I decided to finish putting his laundry away. As I made my way into his closet to hang his clothes, I nearly tripped over the small wooden box again. I dropped the laundry basket I was holding and grabbed the wall to regain my balance.

"You gotta stay focused, or you're gonna fuck this shit up for us."

"You alright in there, gal? Who the hell you talking to?" Mr. Kessler called out to me.

"Yes, I'm fine."

Temptation was a bitch. The money in the box was calling my name, and I was damn sure going to answer it. Maybe this was God finally answering one of my prayers. There was more than enough in the box to pay the remaining balance for my previous semester of school. I decided to take what I needed and more from Mr. Kessler's stash. The old geezer wouldn't miss it. He had plenty of money. Besides, they didn't pay me enough anyway.

With my heart beating out of my chest, I tucked the money I'd stolen down in the laundry basket so I could discreetly transfer it to my purse later. Part of me felt bad for stooping so low, but I had to do what I had to do.

AFTER LEAVING WORK, I SPENT THE LAST THREE HOURS running around to take care of some errands before going home. Hunger was starting to take over, so I stopped by Church's Chicken to grab me something before heading in.

Just as I pulled into the drive through, my phone rang. The sound of my heart beating out of my chest is the only thing I could hear once I saw the name on the screen. The phone shook in my hand as I answered the call.

"Autumn, I need to talk to you," my supervisor Georgette said through the phone. Her tone was serious, and I knew right then she was coming with some shit I didn't need to hear. Just the sound of her voice made my skin crawl.

"Is everything OK?" I asked. The truth is that I already knew why she was calling me. I knew it would only be so long before the dirt I was doing would come back to bury me. And today was the day I had to accept what was coming to me.

"I just got off the phone with Christina Kessler. She says you stole some money from Mr. Kessler's safe."

"What! She's a li–"

"Listen, this is the third time we've had a client say something has come up missing after you've worked a shift. The difference between now and then, is that back then we had no concrete proof. There were too many other people in the mix, so we weren't sure it was you stealing. We gave you the benefit of the doubt. This time we have proof. That makes all the difference. Ms. Kessler has footage of you on the home surveillance system. She's going to send the footage over and says that they are considering pressing charges against you if you don't return the money."

"I don't know what she's talking about. I didn't take any money."

"Autumn, I'm sorry, but Christina Kessler is a big client of ours. I believe her. I'm gonna have to let you go. I'm sorry. You need to give the money back."

"What? You haven't even seen the footage and you're ready to fire me already?" I tried to play innocent until the very end.

My nerves got the best of me. I spent the remainder of my shift with my stomach in knots over what I had done. Even though the voice I heard tried to convince me I'd be in the clear, I pushed Kalidah's voice out of my head. While Mr. Kessler napped, I eased into the closet and put the ten stacks I'd taken back in the box before I left work for the day. I guess that didn't mean shit.

"I'm sorry, Autumn, but I just can't take any chances." Georgette's fat ass hung up the phone in my face. I knew I was wrong for taking the money, but it still didn't sit right with me that I got fired. I did steal in the past, but the first two times was over two years ago when I was going through hard times. Both times, I'd stolen less than two hundred dollars from two of the clients in the facility. I didn't have food in my house, and I needed gas money to last me until my payday. I was in a deep depression, so I'd go shopping to make me feel better. Feeling better meant spending all my bill money and then looking crazy when I couldn't take care of necessities. I met Lucky not long after that while I was in Lennox Mall. He started helping me get on my feet, moved me out of my shitty apartment, and helped me by taking care of the bills so I could focus on school.

Thinking about why I decided to steal from Mr. Kessler made feel stupid. I really had no business and no reason for doing what I did other than the fact that I mismanaged my money. That was on me and my fault. That was the reason I decided to return the money instead of keeping it. The decision to put the money back was hard, but I didn't want to continue to fall victim to my flaws.

"I told you to check behind yourself. This is why you need to listen to me. You need me, Autumn."

43

"Kalidah, leave me the fuck alone! I don't need your help! It's always trouble with you! Shut the fuck up!" I shook my head and returned to my thoughts.

Sometimes the fact that I went without so much when I was younger was the reason why I decided to get the things I wanted now. When Lucky and I were beefing or when I felt down, shopping was my go to therapeutic exercise. I sometimes spent excessively and more than what I could afford to. I was used to Lucky cleaning up my mess, but I knew he was getting tired of me making stupid decisions. He didn't mind giving me money, but he did mind when I would lie about how I spent the money he gave me.

It seemed like shit was getting worse for me by the day. My GiGi is sick and there's nothing I can do about it. I've lost my job. Now, Kalidah wants to show up again.

Chapter Four
Autumn

I woke up to the feeling of Lucky pressing his dick in the back of my ass. It was a welcome feeling, especially since the night before he rejected me. I turned my hips so that he could access my sweet spot with ease. As he slid inside of me, I enjoyed the sensation of his fat, long dick pulsating within my walls.

"You like that?" Lucky asked me.

"Yes," I purred. I rocked my hips to find his rhythm. This is exactly what I wanted. Lucky gripped the back of my neck, pulling my head back enough to caress my neck with his tongue. With his stroke intensifying, I knew it wouldn't be long until he came.

"Get on top of me," I begged him, and he obliged. His strokes increased as my pussy opened up to allow more of him inside. The slickness of my vagina indicated that I was ready for my release. Sensing this, Lucky quickened his pace. We both came at the same time. He splattered his seed inside of me and quickly eased out of me to head to the bathroom to clean himself up.

I got up to meet Lucky in the bathroom. I still hadn't told him that I got fired. It wouldn't change anything as far as who paid the bills, but to be honest I was too embarrassed. I never wanted to be the type of woman who depended on a man for everything. I valued having my own.

"You happy now?" Lucky asked.

"Of course I am."

"I knew all you needed was a lil dick to calm your ass down."

"I need more than just your dick, Lucky. I need your heart, too,"

"You got all that. You just need to chill on all that other shit," Lucky said as he turned on the shower. I decided to hop in with him to clean up.

"What you doing in here?"

"Damn! You don't have to act like that. I'm not going to be in here long anyway. I know how you love your forty-five minute showers. I just want to hit my hot spots right quick."

"You look like you putting on a little weight. In all the right places, though." Lucky slapped my ass and I looked down at myself. My stomach did seem to have a little pudge, but nothing a little exercise couldn't take care of.

I proceeded to wash up so that I could get started with my day. Going up to the Unemployment Office to see if I could find some type of work or get paid for being fired s was a top priority for me since I didn't have anything else to do.

I picked out the most modest outfit I could find in my closet and prepared myself to go down to the unemployment office to grovel my way into the getting my benefits. I needed to have some money coming in. I settled on a classic black pencil skirt, a white silk bow-tie blouse, and the matching jacket.

"Where you going dressed like that? Where your scrubs?" Lucky came into the bedroom wearing only his towel.

"Uhm, I need to go up to the school to take care of a few things," I lied. I wasn't ready to tell him I got fired..

"Aight, I'm gonna head to the barber shop after I get dressed. I'll be home late because I have some shit I need to take care of. You ain't gotta wait up for me."

"Bae, it's some things I need to talk to you about," I said.

"Autumn, that shit is gonna have to wai– I mean, I'll put some time aside to spend some time with you this weekend. I just got a lot of shit going on at the shop right now, and me and June trying to get shit straight."

"Ok." That was all I had in me to say at this point. I no longer wanted to fight. There was too much on my mind right now for me to add another issue between me and Lucky. I had to maintain some sense of normalcy in my life. Especially since it felt like everything else was crashing down around me.

I PULLED UP TO THE UNEMPLOYMENT OFFICE WITH MY heart sitting in my throat. I had no clue as to what I should say to these people to get unemployment benefits. I read something that said it would be difficult for me to get any unemployment money due to the fact that losing my job was my fault.

Pulling out my phone, I called Tamela to see if she had any suggestions. "What's up, girl?" Tam said.

"Girl, I need your help. I'm up here at the Unemployment Office and have no idea what I should say. You know you can sell water to a whale so I figured you could give me something to go with." Her mouth had gotten us out of a lot of trouble over the years.

"Wait! What? You lost your job, Autumn? Damn!"

"Girl, Georgette's fat ass called me after my shift the other day and fired me. She accused me of stealing from Mr. Kessler."

"Damn, for real? Well, did you take from the old fart?"

"Girl, hell n– Well, at first I did take the money, but I couldn't go through with it."

"What in the world possessed your ass to do that?"

"Obviously I need the money! Duh! Not only do I need them three stacks to get back in school, GiGi just found out she has cancer. She can't afford all her medication, and I need to help her. We can talk about all that later, though. I need to know what to say."

"Shit, I don't know. You definitely need to go in there and humble yourself. Tell them about GiGi. Use whatever you have to make them feel sorry for you."

"I hope it works. I need the money until I can find another job. For me and GiGi's sake. Well let me get in here and see what happens."

"Aight then. Call me later and let me know how it goes."

"Ok, girly. I'll hit you up. I may need a drink after this." After disconnecting the call, I got out and adjusted my skirt, grabbed my blazer, and headed in.

Chapter Five
Ezrail

I watched as Autumn sat on the bench outside of the Unemployment Office.

She sat there with tears streaming down her face. Now seemed like the perfect time to introduce her to the plan. She was in a place where she was looking for a savior, and I was prepared to be hers. Not in a Captain-Save-a-Hoe way. Although Autumn was finer than a muhfucker, I had one use for her, and it had nothing to do with sex. She had a gift that she believed was a curse. It was a must that I changed that, though. Soon enough she'd see that the curse she was running from was part of her destiny. Having the gift of multiple personalities would take Autumn far if only she'd embrace it. She could have all the money she needed. It was bigger than her. I needed her to realize the power of the gift she possessed and for her to use that gift to benefit us both.

Positioning was key, though. I continued watching Autumn, deciding how I would approach her. She was in a delicate situation, and I knew I needed to use that to my advantage. I would do just that. Mastering the art of manipulation is what earned me the trust of the others and why I was the perfect person to recruit new people to my team. My skills for bringing new recruits up to speed was unmatched. My only concern at this point was Alya. I never knew what her next move would be, but that made the game more intriguing.

I watched as Autumn wiped the tears from her face. She pulled her phone from her purse to answer an incoming call. A look of concern spread across her face as she tried to compose herself enough to answer. I knew it was a call about her grandmother and what she would hear on the other line would nearly break her spirit.

"Timing can't get any better than this," I said to himself. I placed a Newport between my thick lips, lit it, and inhaled the rich flavor of the tobacco. Today seemed like the perfect day to change a life, but I thought better of it. Hopefully another opportunity would come soon for me to give Autumn my proposition. I needed to play my hand properly.

Chapter Six
Alya

Telling Autumn that I could not approve her unemployment claim was very hard, but necessary for me I needed to set the tone for the way forward and blocking her from the opportunity to pursue one of the desires of her heart was necessary. But delay was not denial and if Autumn made the right decision, she would have access to all the things she dreamed of and more eventually.

I watched Autumn from my office window as I sipped the white chocolate mocha coffee I picked up on her way in. I knew Autumn would be visiting the office that day and wanted to try to prepare myself for the conversation that needed to be had. Letting people down was never something I took lightly, and this situation with Autumn was no different.

"Ms. Alya, are you finished with the files on your desk? I'd like to return them to the records room," my assistant, Mariah, asked.

"Yes, I'm done with all the files except the Carrington file. I'll need this one a while longer."

"Ok, no worries. Please let me know if I can get you anything else."

"Can you clear my schedule tomorrow afternoon? Cancel all of my meetings. There's something I need to take care of."

"Sure, you got it," Mariah said as she left the office. My attention returned to my window where Ezrail had just come into view. I watched him as he watched Autumn. It was clear to me that he would be making his move sooner rather than later. I was okay with that, though. It could give me time to gain more intel on what Ezrail's plan may be. I knew whatever it was would be difficult for Autumn to refuse; however, I'd also present Autumn with something beneficial to her. Something I felt would also help her grow as a person. She needed to know that she didn't have to run from who she was, and I wanted to show her how to overcome the things she felt she needed to hide.

"Hang on, baby girl. You'll get to be all that you want to be in due time," I whispered to myself. I knew I would have to close in soon in order to secure Autumn for my team. I hated losing to Ezrail, and there was no denying he was powerful. The truth, however, was that he would never be able to measure up to me and the unique power I possessed. It was time to show Autumn how to conquer her fears so that she could be all that she desired and more.

Chapter Seven
Autumn

Storming out of the Unemployment Office with my tears blinding me, I took a seat on a nearby bench. I needed to compose myself because what I received in the office was rejection. Once again. And the sting of it, no matter where it came from, always seemed to take a heavy toll on me.

"Autumn you already knew the count. I can help you fix this if you let me."

"Don't start that shit! Just shut up!" I said aloud. I glanced around to see if anyone was watching me and saw my outburst. Thankfully, there was no one around. My phone rang. I looked down to see GiGi calling. Swiping tears from my face and clearing my throat, I answered the phone. "Hey GiGi, how are you feeling?"

"I'm ok, baby. I'm hanging in there. I got some more bad news. Some of the cancer has already spread to my lymph nodes. They pushing my surgery up, and I just wanted to let you know. It's gonna be in two days. You think you can make it? I know you have to work, but I would love it if all my babies could be there with me."

"This sounds serious, GiGi, so of course I'll be there. I love you so much, and I just can't lose yo–"

"Wait a minute, baby. Who said I was going anywhere? I still got a lot of life to live. Don't you go putting me in no grave yet. Didn't I tell you God has already healed me? I just need the love of God and all my babies surrounding me when I have my surgery."

"I'm sorry, GiGi. You mean so much to me, and I'm just so thankful for you."

"I know, baby. I'm so proud of you. You hear me?"

"Yes, ma'am" I whispered.

"Ok. Well, let me get ready to go. I need to get ready to watch my stories. *Young and the Restless* is coming on in five minutes."

"Talk to you later, GiGi. Love you."

"Love you, too, baby. Talk to ya later."

After I hung up with GiGi, the tears continued to flow. The fact that the only person who had ever been there for me was facing a life-threatening illness weighed heavily on me. I wanted to believe that GiGi would be ok, but I just couldn't. I prayed she would be ok, but I didn't have faith like GiGi did. Stage Two cancer was serious, and with each stage the mortality rate increased.

I decided to call Lucky, but of course, he didn't answer his phone. This had been his mode of operation lately and I was tired of it.

"He don't give a shit about you. You been knowing that, boo. When you gone stop being a victim? I'm waiting for you to let me do what I need to do. Remember the promise?"

"Shit!" I got up and headed to my car, still in a daze. I didn't see the man coming toward me through the haze of my tears. As a result, we bumped into each other. Our eyes met. I immediately recognized him as the man I saw coming into my building the other night. Once again, his presence sent chills through me. At the same time, I was intrigued. His broad nose, thick chocolate lips, and powerful energy captured me.

"My bad," he said.

"It's cool." Feeling embarrassed, I hurried to my car. I couldn't take my eyes off the man as he vanished to the other side of the parking lot.

I SPENT THE REST OF THE AFTERNOON AT LENNOX MALL and Phipps Plaza shopping, spending money I didn't have. Even though my checking account was screaming for me to give it a rest, I needed a pick me up. The Gucci store had just what I needed in the form of a black crossbody with a gold chain. The joy I felt from the purchase was temporary, but it did what I needed it to do at the time.

After calling Lucky several times all day with no answer, I decided to pull up on him at the barber shop. After the way he fucked me this morning, I felt like things were finally getting back on track. It was now about eight o'clock at night, and he hadn't checked in. His car was in the parking lot along with a white Hyundai Sonata, but the shop appeared to be dark.

I didn't bother to call Lucky to let him know I was there. Unbeknownst to him, I made a copy of the key to the shop, so I let myself in. Quietly, I tiptoed towards the back of the shop to Lucky's office. Soft moans filled the air, causing rage to pulsate within my veins. I yanked the door of the office open to find Lucky seated in his chair with the bitch, Whitney, butt naked riding him like a rodeo cowgirl! The smell of fresh pussy filled the air.

Without thinking, I charged Whitney, grabbing her by her hair and pulling her up off my man. I drew my fist back as far as I could and rammed it into her face. Lucky jumped up, stuffing his wet dick back into his pants.

"So you still fucking with a man that will never make you his number one?" I smashed her head into Lucky's desk. She slid down to the floor, giving me the perfect opportunity to introduce her to the pair of black, heeled combat boots I was wearing.

"Autumn, calm the fuck down!" Lucky screamed as he grabbed me from behind in an effort to get me off Whitney.

"Get the fuck off me, bitch!" Whitney flapped her arms like she was swimming, but none of her hits landed. The blood that released from her nose when I kicked her in her face rested above her lips

"Nah, bitch! Nah, bitch! You been had this shit coming! You lucky I don't kill your ass right here!" I screamed. Lucky finally succeeded at pulling me off her. I turned around and slapped him so hard that he stood there wearing my handprint on his face.

"You wanna kill me and not the nigga who keeps choosing

me?" She hurriedly found the dress she was wearing and slid it over her body.

"Shut the fuck up, Whitney! Both of you bitches need to shut up! Damn!" Lucky yelled. Part of me wanted to end Lucky's life tonight. I was tired of him playing me.

"See, you playing. Why don't you just let me go ahead and take care of this nigga right now?"

"Fuck you!" I grabbed the first thing that I could find, which was a paperweight, and hurled it at Lucky's head.

"Bitch, calm the fuck down! You ain't got too many more opportunities to put your hands on me. This shit be the main reason why a nigga out here with this bitch! Whitney, just get your shit and go. I'll get with you later."

"You'll get with her later?" I repeated.

"Yeah, you heard what the fuck I said!" Lucky belted. He walked up on me like he wanted to hurt me.

"Yeah you heard him bit–" Whitney said.

"Bitch shut the fuck up!" I charged toward her once again, but Lucky lifted me off the ground and placed me in the same chair he was just sitting in. Whitney sauntered out the door with a smirk on her face and the cheap wig she wore cocked on the side of her head. This wouldn't be the last she saw of me. I wasn't done with her.

Deep in my soul, I felt defeated and humiliated. I knew all along Lucky was fucking around on me, but catching him did something to me. It left the type of pain in my heart that reminded me of the pain my mother inflicted on me.

"Autumn, this shit is dead. I can't do this anymore," Lucky said, brazenly.

"Don't start that bullshit. Now you want to act like I'm the problem when the whole time you been cheating?" I asked.

"You're just not someone I feel I can build with. I am tired of trying to force something that just ain't meant to be. We should have just stayed fuck buddies instead of taking shit as far as we did," he coldly replied.

"What the fuck you mean? You can't do this anymore? You just gonna walk away from me like this after all I've done for you? After taking two years of my life?"

"This shit been over. You finally pushed me to do what you kept accusing me of doing. You've become more of a liability than an asset, and a nigga is done. My patience with you has run out."

"You can't be fucking serious right now. The whole time you been playing in my face! The whole time you been making me think I was just tripping when you round here sticking your dick in another bitch! The same bitch I caught you with before, and I'm the problem?"

"She provides what you don't– a clean house, hot meals, and good sex. I mean, ain't shit wrong with your sex game. It's the other shit that fucks up the vibe. She don't nag me like you do."

"Wow! Tell me how you really feel. You just think I ain't shit, huh? Nothing I've ever done for you matters."

"I'm not saying that. It's just that you're not the one for me. I've done just as much for you and you definitely don't show me no fucking appreciation. You think sex is enough to keep a nigga, and that's where you gonna go wrong every time."

"So now what am I supposed to do since you've decided I'm not the one for you? I came up here to talk to you because I lost my job yesterday. I got so much shit on my mind! I can't get back in school, my GiGi has cancer, and now you want to fucking leave me?"

"Look, I'm sorry to hear about GiGi and that you lost your job. As far as you not being able to get back in school, that shit's on you. But if it makes you feel any better, I'll bring you some money to cover the rent up for the next two months."

"That's all you got to say to me?" Anger was raging inside of me. Lucky was being way too nonchalant for me. He had the audacity to stand in front of me ridiculing me when he was the one who was fucking up our relationship all along.

"What else you want me to say?"

"You're right. You've said enough as it is."

"Oh, I got all my clothes from the house, so you don't have to worry about me coming by. I'll call to let you know when to come pick up the money for the rent."

I felt humiliated. Tears welled up in my eyes as the pain I felt gave way to anger. I stormed out of Lucky's office and grabbed a broom that was resting on the wall outside of the door. I smashed every mirror at every barber station on my way out and proceeded to do the same to the window of Lucky's Mercedes Benz S550. I heard Lucky's footsteps trailing behind, but I didn't give a fuck! I kept it pushing out the front door and headed to my car.

"Yo! What the fuck did you just do?" He was now outside the shop door yelling at me. "You're one crazy bitch! You know that!" I ignored him and hopped into my car. My tires screeched as I sped away from the barber shop and onto the highway.

"Was that all you had? You should have killed him and that

dirty hoe he was with. One day you gone listen to me. We'll show him what a crazy bitch really looks like."

I turned up the radio. The sound of H.E.R.'s song "Trauma" helped to drown out the voice in my head.

Chapter Eight
Autumn

S even days passed since Lucky left me. Darkness filled my apartment and co-mingled with the heaviness of my grief. It weighed on me and held me hostage. I hadn't left my apartment since, nor had I eaten anything or slept. My thick, curly hair sat atop my head in a knotty bun that resembled a bird's nest.

"Look at you! You're pathetic!" Kalidah said.

"Kalidah, leave me the fuck alone! All you're doing is making shit worse! Keeping me up all night with your bullshit!"

I got up from my bed to relieve myself. The putrid smell of seven days' worth of piss and shit nearly knocked me on my back when I pulled my pants down to pee. I didn't care. I had no reason to fix myself up, nor did I feel like it. I finished peeing, pulled my funky, piss-tinged panties up, flushed the toilet, and headed back to my bed.

I buried my head into Lucky's pillow and inhaled the scent of his cologne. Tears filled the wells of my eyes once again, but I tried to force them back. Tired of crying would be an under-statement for how I felt, but I couldn't stop the tears from flowing.

"So you really gonna sit here and keep crying over this nigga? I tried to protect you from this, Ms. Girl, but you always gotta think you running something! You gotta stop trying to hide me. I made a promise to help you and my word is my bond."

My phone buzzed. Before I looked down to see who was calling me, I whispered a prayer. "Lord, if you can hear me, please let whoever this is calling me be Lucky." Slowly opening my eyes, I looked down to see Tamela's name on my screen. I didn't want to talk to her right now, so I sent her to voicemail. There were about thirty-two notifications and missed calls on my phone. They were mostly from Tamela, but I did have a few calls from GiGi.

My heart sank because I hadn't been to see GiGi yet. I knew she was probably worried about me because she knew whenever I went missing, something was wrong. I listened to the message she left on my phone and was surprised to hear my mother's voice instead of GiGi's.

"Hey Sugar Baby – I, uh, mean Autumn– this is your mo– This is Winter. Mama wanted me to reach out to you. Well, actually, uh, I've been wanting to call you myself, but, uh, anyway, mama had her surgery. She was worried about you since you didn't show up. She's still in the hospital but should be coming home this evening. Call me back. Bye."

Letting GiGi down broke my heart. I promised myself that if I could pull myself out of this funk today, then I would be over her house first thing in the morning. I couldn't let her see me like this, though. She would see right through me, and I didn't want to put any additional stress on her.

I scrolled through the rest of my missed calls and wished Lucky's name would have been there. Of course it wasn't there. Lucky completely severed all ties with me. True to his word, all his belongings were gone. Today was the first day I hadn't called his phone, but that didn't mean I wouldn't before the end of the day.

I closed my eyes and tried to remember the good times between me and Lucky, but those memories were overpowered by all the times I caught him cheating in the past. Being the master manipulator he was, he somehow convinced me that my suspicions about him cheating were just due to my insecurities. I turned over to try to quiet my mind and drift to sleep, but the sound of someone banging on my front door ruined the moment.

"Autumn! Autumn! Open this damn door! I know you're in there! If you don't open this muhfucking door right now, I'm gonna call the police to bust this bitch down," Tamela screamed.

I got up and headed to the living room to open the door. Pausing there, I looked around my apartment and realized that in the last seven days, I'd managed to destroy all my hard work from cleaning the other day. My apartment was trashed, but by the sounds of the way Tam was carrying on, I decided to open the door anyway.

"Why the fuck are you out here knocking on my fucking door like you're the police?" I questioned as I swung the door open.

"Bitch, as if you don't know why. I thought your ass was up

in here dead. I've been calling you, and your ass hasn't been answering the motherfucking phone!"

"Y'all good out here?" I heard a deep voice asked. My eyes locked in on his. I had to look away. When I saw him a couple of days ago on campus, I knew I'd seen him somewhere before, but didn't realize then that he was the new guy who moved into my building. What's the odds that he'd actually live across the hall from me? I didn't even realize the neighbors across the hall moved and their apartment was available for lease.

"Yes. We're ok," I hesitantly responded. Mr. Mysterious looked back at me and went back in his apartment. "Girl, get your ass in here before somebody calls the police on us."

"So I gotta beat your door down for you to answer my calls?" Tamela bellowed. "And you need to clean this nasty ass–"

"Watch your fucking mouth. I know my apartment is dirty. I don't need you to remind me. Keep in mind that you brought your ass over here to my house without an invite. Tread lightly with the disrespect."

"Girl, fuck you! I ain't trying to hear none of that bullshit you're talking right now. I came over here out of concern for you and your family. They've been blowing up my phone, asking me to get a welfare check started."

"I'm fine. I'm just going through some things, and I don't want to be bothered."

"Shit, I already know it's about Lucky."

"Yeah. And...?"

"Look, you ain't going to keep talking to me crazy! Now you know I love you, but you gotta get yourself together. A nigga leaving you ain't the end of the world. Just like you got him, you can get another. I been told you that nigga wasn't shit, but I wasn't gonna keep talking to you about it. It was up to you to realize that shit."

"Tam, I don't need your 'I told you so.' You can save that shit. I'm gonna go see my grandmother today. I don't want her to continue to worry about me."

"That's the least you could do. You putting all this unnecessary stress on your grandmother that she doesn't need right now."

"Damn! I get it. You don't have to keep telling me!"

"I'm not trying to beat your head in with my opinion. I just think you deserve better than this. Your dreams didn't die when Lucky left. You can still accomplish your goals, but the first thing we need you to do is take your funky ass in your bathroom and get in the shower. Matter of fact , you need to soak your ass in the bathtub first. Put some bleach and some more shit in the water."

"Bitch, fuck you!" I laughed. Shit, Tam wasn't lying. Before I even attempted to go to GiGi's house, I needed to make sure my ass was squeaky clean. Any indication that I was struggling or in a depressed state would put my grandmother in a state of worry.

"Look, I can come back over here later and help you clean this shit when you come back from GiGi's house if you want, but I can't stay too long. I got a date tonight.

"Girl, don't even worry about it. I can clean my own house. I don't need your help with that."

"OK, so now that I know you're OK, I'm gonna go. I'll call your fam to let them know you're good."

"Aight. I'm gonna go soak my funky ass in a bleach filled tub like you suggested." I laughed for the first time in days.

"Well, I'll call you later to check on you. Just make sure you let me know how you're doing and let your fam know so they don't keep worrying about you. Oh, I almost forgot, Perry Staffing Solutions is holding interviews for job openings they have. It's a temp agency, so they will probably be able to help you find something. Here's the card I picked up," Tam handed me a small blue and white business card. "Give them a call to set something up. At least it will help you have some income coming in until everything else works itself out."

"Thanks, girl. Now get out of here. I'll call you tomorrow." I shooed Tam out the door because to be honest, I had enough of her presence. I needed to get my mind right before I went to my granny's house.

I decided with the way my body odor was now set up that it would definitely serve me well to take Tam's advice and soak in a bath minus the bleach. While the water filled the tub, I rummaged through the dirty clothes that littered my closet floor to find something clean or at least something that didn't smell to put on.

"You'll feel better when you let us help you. I don't know why you try to suppress us. We only want to share your life."

Chapter Nine
Autumn

I pulled up to my granny's house to check on her. With the revelation of her breast cancer diagnosis and the fact that I missed her surgery, my heart was heavy. As I approached the front door, my mind raced. All I wanted was for GiGi to be okay. The thought of losing her nearly suffocated me. I sucked in large gulps of air as I tried to calm myself, but the shaking of my hands and heart racing wouldn't let me. I loved my grandmother so much for stepping up when my mother couldn't. She was as solid as they came and she did not play about family. That's why I always made it my business to make sure she was good. Or, at least, I tried to. Most would say that I was failing at that at this point. Gigi was the glue that had always held this family together. I didn't know what I would do without her.

"Hey there, Sugar baby," Granny greeted me as I entered her small three-bedroom house. "Come on in here and set down with me." GiGi led me to the small kitchen. GiGi's kitchen was neat and clean. White lace valances hung from the kitchen window. GiGi's love for red apples was evident throughout the space. They were on the rugs, hand towels, and placemats on the small wooden table that was in the corner of the small kitchen. Seeing how pristine GiGI kept her home would make you wonder what happened to me. She loved a clean home. It seemed I loved chaos.

"I just wanted to stop by and check on you," I said as I stopped and hugged her. "Shouldn't you be laying down somewhere?"

"Oh baby, I'm alright. I go back to the doctor tomorrow to get some more tests done, and for the doctor to see how I'm healing." She replied.

"Do you need me to take you? I can call out of work tomorrow," I said. There was no way I was gonna let Gigi know I was jobless.

"Naw, baby. That's alright. Your Aunt Tweety said she'd go ahead and take me. How are you doing? We were worried about you. It ain't like you not to come around for me."

"I know, GiGi, I'm sorry. Time got away from me." I tried to avoid making eye contact with GiGi because I knew if I did, she'd know I was lying. It didn't take much for her to see through me.

"Well, you look like you putting on a little weight. Your stomach is looking a lil' thick. At least I know you eating good. And you look tired. You know you need to make sure you're getting all your rest. You been taking your medication? You know what happens if you don't." Gigi looked at me with concern on her face.

"I don't need no medication, GiGi. I'm fine. I promise."

"Is everything alright with you and Lucky? I tried calling him, too, when we were looking for you, but he never did return my call."

"Everything is fine, GiGi. Lucky has been out of town for about a week now, so that's probably why he didn't answer." GiGi eyed me suspiciously. Whenever she looked at me like that, I knew she wasn't buying nothing I was saying. "Now enough about me. Why ain't you in bed? Where is Aunt Tweety?"

"Oh, I been resting all day, but you know me. I asked the good Lord to give me strength to get up and move around. When you lay around too long, you're killing yourself. I gotta keep moving so I can stay alive for a long time. And, Tweety is at work right now. She'll be over here later."

"Well, I just wanted to stop by and apologize to you. Come on, let me walk you back to your room so you can get some rest." I got up to help GiGi out of her seat. We headed down the hallway to her small master bedroom. After removing the pillows, I pulled the yellow lace bedspread back so GiGi could get in.

"Autumn? Is that you?" I turned around to see my mother standing in the doorway. The sight of her caught me off guard. Even though the drugs and her sickness had plagued her most of her life, she still looked beautiful. A gray streak of hair ran through the front left side of her long dark hair. It complimented her toffee colored complexion. Even though she was on the thin side, she still possessed a nice physique.

"Hey, Winter." I still couldn't bring myself to call her mom. She'd never done anything motherly other than push me out of her pussy.

"Are you ok? We were all worried about you. I thought maybe you'd, uhm, I thought that something bad may have happened to you or maybe you'd had an episode."

"Oh so you thought maybe I was like you? You thought I was in my apartment talking to the voices in my head and getting high?"

"That's not what I'm saying, sweetie, but you know you can't keep running from your truth." Winter came into the room and approached me with her arms open to hug me. My muscles briefly tensed up. Without realizing what I was doing, I instantly pushed her hands away. It was something about her trying to hug me that rubbed me the wrong way. Especially now. Years ago, I would have done just about anything for that hug, but today, not so much.

"Autumn, who you talking to like that?" GiGi asked. "You don't need to be carrying on like that around me."

"I'm sorry, GiGi. I really am."

"Baby, I think you need to get you some rest when you go back home. I can tell you ain't been sleeping good. You can go ahead and gone home. Tweety will be here soon, and your mama will be here until then."

"Ok, well, I'll call you later on," I said leaning in to kiss GiGi on her cheek. "Bye, GiGi."

"See ya later, baby," GiGi responded. I brushed past Winter like she wasn't there. She didn't say a word to me, even though I'm sure she wanted to.

Whisper When You Say My Name

On my way home, I decided to stop by Lucky's barbershop. Even though I'd called him multiple times, he wouldn't answer my calls. He was still mad at me about how I acted the other night. And, rightfully so, but I was also justified in my anger. I needed that money he said he would give me for the rent.

I spotted Lucky's car as soon as I pulled into the parking lot. It was still sitting there with the busted windows. This was surprising to me because Lucky loved that car.

I checked my reflection in the mirror before I hopped out of the car. The wetness of the palms of my hands caused my hand to slip slightly when I pulled the door handle to the barbershop. My stomach tightened as I walked into the shop. As usual, men were scattered throughout the shop waiting to get their hair cut.

As soon as Joe's big ass saw me, a smirk appeared on his face. I could tell the type of energy he was on. If I had it my way, I would punch the shit out of him. But I knew I was no match for his big, burly ass.

"Here come that crazy bitch!" Joe said loud enough for everyone and their mama to hear.

"Smash his fucking head in."

"Fuck you say, bitch?" Joe asked.

"So, I guess you really feeling yourself today, Joe? Don't get fucked up in here like I fucked up this shop! Where the fuck is Lucky? I need to talk to him."

"See, that's why Lucky don't fuck with your ass right now! You don't know how to stay in a female's place," Joe said as he stood there glaring at me. I wanted nothing more than to take the sharpest object I could find and Ram it in his throat.

"Girl, let me fuck this fat bitch up. I'm sure ain't nobody

checking for his ass anyway. I promise, if I had my way his ass would be a distant memory..."

"Fuck you, you fat, greasy motherfucker!" I said as June approached me, trying to diffuse the situation.

"Autumn, I think you should leave. Don't come in here making a scene. Now ain't the time for you to see Lucky," June said. He grabbed me by the arm and walked me back outside.

"Look, Autumn, I'm only telling you this because I care about you, shawty, but don't come up here no more. Lucky will be here soon and he ain't over the shit you did in here a few days ago. Trust me, you need to let him air out a little while longer," June advised.

For some reason, I broke down crying. I finally fucked shit up big time between Lucky and I. My life was crumbling around me. My hopes, my dreams, everything. To add to that, mentally I was breaking, too. Kalidah refused to leave me alone. Taunting me and whispering things to me in my head.

"Shawty, never let a nigga see you sweat. Lucky is my boy and all but he's been playing you right in your face for too long. The problem with you is that you've given Lucky too much power over you. He's made you a pawn in his game, and he don't even deserve to have you. Adjust your crown, shawty. Take your power back."

"It's not that easy, June. We're engaged. We're supposed to get married and have a couple of kids. We're supposed to be a power couple on next level shit in the streets of Atlanta," I said between sobs.

"Aye, I get all that, but you need to think about something. If Lucky was pressed about you the same way you pressed about him, you wouldn't be standing here right now with tears in your eyes. Just remember this, never let a nigga tell you twice that he don't want you. My grandmother used to tell my sisters that all the time. Lucky showed you what it is. Now, you need to get on outta here before Lucky pulls up."

"You're right. Thanks for not letting me continue to make a fool of myself. Truth be told, I wanted to smash Joe's head in, but I don't want to give his fat ass anything else to say about me."

"Don't worry about that nigga. He just mad because he ain't getting no pussy or no play from you." June gave me a hug and walked me to my car. I sat there for a moment before I pulled off trying to get my mind together. The constant racing of my mind was starting to affect everything and the voices were starting to make me look stupid.

As I sat there trying to compose myself, a blue BMW three series pulled up to the shop. I watched as Lucky and Whitney hopped out of the car and made a mental note of her license plate number. I had a photographic memory and would have no problem recalling the number when I needed it at a later time. Whitney kissed Lucky before getting into the driver's seat and pulling off. June was still out there, and he glanced in my direction without making it obvious. Anger boiled inside of me, but I knew now was not the time to do anything. While it seemed like Lucky this was truly the end for me and Lucky, it surely wouldn't be the last time he'd see me. At some point he would understand how him fucking me over affected me. Him and that new bitch of his would have to answer for the pain in my heart.

Chapter Ten
Autumn

It was seven o'clock in the morning when I woke up to realize I would be late to the temp agency if I didn't haul ass to get ready. Jumping up from the coziness of my bed, I hopped in the shower to rinse off quickly. A wave of nausea hit me and forced me out of the shower and on my knees in front of my toilet. Once I was finished vomiting, I hopped back in the shower to clean up and quickly got out to dry off. I threw on the black suit I picked out the night before, grabbed my purse, and headed out the door.

As I approached my car, it looked like it was leaning a bit on one side. I said a prayer that my worst fear in this moment was not coming true. The last thing I needed was anything to slow me down from getting where I needed to go. Obviously, my prayers still didn't reach God's ears because a flat tire greeted me as I walked to the driver's side of the car.

"Shit!" I yelled and proceeded to kick the side of my Benz.

Tears streamed down my face. It seemed like catching a break was not in the cards for me. I pulled out my phone and called Tamela to see if she could pick me up, but as luck would have it, she didn't answer.

"Yo, you good, ma?" I looked up to see my neighbor from across the hall peering at me through the passenger side window of his car. The smell of his cologne floated through the air and reached my nose. The scent was familiar. In an instant, memories of Lucky flooded my mind. If he was here right now, all of my current problems would have been solved.

"You know what? Nah, I'm not good. Far from it!" I said, pointing to the flat tire that was threatening to derail my day.

"You got a spare? I might be able to help" he asked as he stepped out of his car and approached me. I wondered just what he was going to do wearing a nice pair of designer jeans, a black sweater, and black Timberland boots. Clearly, he was dressed a little too nice to be doing dirty work.

"Spare? Where would I find the spare?" I didn't know shit about no damn cars or where the spare tire was located even though I knew it was something I should have been aware of. In the past, Lucky took care of anything I needed done to the car.

"Pop your trunk. It's probably in there." I did as I was told. He obviously knew more than me. Pulling back the carpet layer in the trunk, he removed a latch to a door that revealed the spare tire.

"What's your name anyway? I keep seeing you, but you never introduce yourself. Seems you're always popping up when I'm in some kind of distress."

He pulled his head from my trunk and turned around to lean on the car. "Ezrail...what's yours?"

"Autumn," I said. Ezrail had captivating looks. He was attractive and most women would have been happy to have him there rescuing them from their distress. He wasn't my cup of tea, though. I only had eyes for Lucky, still.

"Seems like you're always in some shit, Autumn. And this spare tire ain't no good. You gonna have to get a new one. Where you need to go?"

"I have a job interview at a temp agency on the other side of town. Then I need to go up to my school to see how I could settle this balance so I can get back in class."

"So, you looking for work?"

"Yeah, basically, or at least a way to earn enough money to take care of my necessities for a while."

"I see. Well, check it, you ain't gone be able to go nowhere without a ride. I can take you where you need to go. I ain't got shit to do right now so it wouldn't be a problem."

"Look, I don't even know you like that. You could be an ax murderer or some shit." I took in the smirk he wore on his face.

"Well, I'm not exactly an ax murderer, but I ain't afraid to get my hands dirty if necessary. Relax, Ma. I ain't here to take your life, but maybe I can help change it."

"Help change it how?" The only thing that would change my life right now would be two things–getting Lucky back and somebody handing me enough paper to change my circumstances. Ezrail damn sure wasn't the one who could help me with either.

"By giving you a ride to where you need to go." Ezrail popped the old spare tire back into its compartment in the trunk and headed to his car. He opened my door. I reluctantly got in. It wasn't like I had too many other options and I needed to get this job.

"Plug the address to where I need to take you," he said, pointing to the large screen in the middle of the dashboard.

"I saw you a few days ago," I said as I did as he asked. We exited the apartment complex and headed towards the highway.

"You saw me? Where you see me at, Ma?" he quizzed.

"I knew you looked familiar when I saw you here in the complex, but I couldn't put my finger on where I saw you before that. Then it dawned on me that I saw you outside the unemployment office the other day. You looking for work or something?"

"Nah, I ain't looking for work. At least not the kind of work they offering at the unemployment office. An old friend of mine works there. I just dropped by to see her."

"An old friend, huh? Oh ok. Well since you volunteered yourself to take me to the temp agency, do you think you can run me past the campus, too? I promise I won't be long. I got a message from the financial aid department, and I need to talk to someone there."

"I got you. Like I said earlier, I ain't got much planned for the day. I'm a night owl anyway. That's usually the time I'm out and about handling my business."

"So that would explain why it seems like I mostly run into you in the wee hours of the morning when you're coming in or at night when you're leaving. You work nights somewhere?"

"Yeah, you could say that." That smirk appeared on his face once again. Smiles like his were used to hypnotize people into doing things they shouldn't be doing. There was something about him that spelled charm and mystery, and I kinda liked it.

"So where ya man at, Autumn?"

"My *fiancé* is out of town," I lied as I flashed him the engagement ring I still wore. I pulled the sun visor down to block the brightness of the sun that was violating my eyes.

"Oh excuse me, *your fiancé*. He got that barbershop in Decatur down on Snapfinger, right?"

"Yeah, he do." I shifted uncomfortably in my seat. I had a feeling he was going to tell me he saw Lucky and that he knew I was lying.

"Oh word, I been there a few times. Haven't been in a while. Look, though, when I finish running you around to wherever you need to go, I can take you by the tire shop and grab you a used tire. You gone need that if you plan on getting around. Especially since your fiancé is out of town right now."

"Oh, you don't have to worry about doing all that. I'll make sure I get that taken care of."

"You sure? It ain't no thing for me to do that."

"I'll let you know." We pulled into the shopping center where the temp agency was, and I hopped out. Smoothing the front of my blouse, I headed toward the door. When I entered, an older white woman was sitting at the desk popping a piece of chewing gum. The closer I got to her, the more the scent of White Diamonds became apparent.

"Can I help you?" the woman asked.

"Uh, yes. I, uh– My name is Autumn Carrington, and I have an interview."

"Sign in right here and have a seat."

I sat down in the hard folding chair they had in the shabby

waiting room. A paint chip from the peeling wall `fell and landed on my shoulder. I felt like that was a sign that I needed to get up and get my ass out of there. I couldn't believe my life had come down to this. Imagine me sitting in the office of a temp agency trying to get work because I fucked around and got fired...

"Ms. Carrington." I looked up to see a young white woman standing near the receptionist's desk holding a manila file folder.

"That's me," I said as I got up and headed in her direction.

"I'm Lindsay. We're just going to go right in here." I trailed behind her to a small office. The scent of what smelled like corn chips and ass cheese hit my nose and instantly made my stomach swirl. I tried to play it off as Lindsay directed me to have a seat at a small table.

"So, typically we do an informal interview, and I go over what opportunities we currently have that would meet your skill set. So, I see that you were working as a nursing assistant at your last job. Can you tell me what happened with that?"

"Well, uh. Well, they decided to let me go. They were making some staffing changes."

"Staffing changes. You sure about that, Ms. Carrington? You know we do reference checks before you even get in here. I was hoping you would be honest with me."

"So, if you already know why I was fired, why are you wasting my damn time then? You either have a job for me or you don't," I said as I stood up.

"Well, I see why they let you go. I wanted to give you the opportunity to tell me the truth. We give second chances around here, especially when applicants own their truth.

Clearly you haven't reached that level of accountability and maturity. Furthermore, I decline to hire anyone who feels it's ok to walk into an interview and speak the way you do."

"You know what, whatever! Fuck you, lady! I don't have time for this shit!" I threw my crossbody over my shoulder and hauled ass out of there with the remaining dignity that I had. I just blew an opportunity because I let my temper flare up. I'd been doing a lot of that lately.

"You should have throat punched that pale ass bitch! She could have used a little color, and a black eye would have suited her nicely."

"Shit you 're probably right!" I busted out laughing, but quickly remembered that I was outside, heading toward Ezrail's car. I looked around to see if anyone saw my little show. Concealing my colorful personality was getting harder and harder. I opened the door to Ezrail's car and hopped in wondering if he'd saw me talking to myself.

"So how that shit work out for you in there?" Ezrail inquired as I closed the car door.

"It didn't," I dryly responded. Ezrail cranked up the car, and we pulled off. He was silent for a minute. He didn't press me for more details. I was thankful for that, considering we didn't know each other like that.

"So, who were you talking to? And why'd your voice sound different?" Ezrail asked. I shifted in my seat and gently chewed on the bottom of my lip.

"Huh? What are you talking about?" I knew my dumb act wasn't it, but it was worth a try.

"I heard you talking. Wasn't sure if you were on the phone or something." He eyed me suspiciously.

"Yeah, I was on the phone. It was my fiancé checking in. I was just impersonating how that lady was talking to me when I went in there." I didn't know why I felt the need to be lying right now, but it was what it was.

"Autumn, you ain't gotta lie to me. I ain't here to judge, but I hear you sometimes over there in your apartment."

"Whatchu mean you be hearing me? You standing at my door spying on me? Don't tell me you be on that weird shit."

"Weird shit might be right, but just know I know your kind. It ain't shit to be ashamed of though."

"My kind? What the fuck is that supposed to even mean? Yeah, you definitely on some weird shit."

"You hear voices and sometimes the voices project themselves through you. I had an auntie like that. She was smart as fuck and loved to paint."

"I don't know what the fuck you're talking about, but you obviously got me fucked up. I ain't like your crazy auntie. And you don't know what you talking about." I nervously chomped down on my bottom lip, causing the taste of my blood to fill my mouth.

"Aight. Imma let this one rock, but just know, I see you. You ain't gotta hide that shit around me. Amazing things can happen when you embrace all of you. Owning your shit will be way more beneficial to you than your shit owning you. Just think about that."

I couldn't say shit else. There was no one who knew my secret but some of my close family. And I wasn't about to admit to Ezrail that he was right. I felt some kind of way about a stranger knowing more about me than some of those closest to me.

The remainder of the ride was silent. My embarrassment wouldn't let me say anything else. It was crazy to me how you could just meet a person and they know you without really knowing you. Ezrail was that person and for some reason, I had a feeling that he understood me more than anybody ever would.

Chapter Eleven
Autumn

I walked into the Unemployment Office with the hopes that I would be able to finally get benefits until I found another job. The other day, I received a message from Ms. Alya Thomas saying that she may be able to help me get what I needed. I hoped like hell she would be able to deliver.

I approached the receptionist's desk, signed in, then took a seat in the waiting room. My phone chimed, alerting me to a message. Wishing it was Lucky professing his love for me, I sighed when I saw that it was Tamela.

Tamela, 9:27 am: *Hey girl. Got your message. Had to go into work early. I can take you where you need to go tomorrow. I'm off so it won't be a problem.*

I didn't even bother to text Tam back right away. In all honesty, my mind was all over the place. My mind racing day in and day out was becoming a frequent thing for me lately. I spent a lot of days accomplishing little because the busyness of my mind stagnated me more than it motivated me.

"Ms. Carrington, Ms. Thomas is ready for you," the receptionist said, breaking my thoughts. Stuffing my phone inside of my purse, I hopped up.

"She's in the last office on the right."

"Ok, thank you." I headed down the hall. Reaching Ms. Thomas's office, I lightly tapped.

"Ms. Carrington, come on in." she said, extending her hand for me to shake it.

"Nice to see you again, Ms. Thomas," I replied. My earlier interaction with Lindsay crossed my mind and I decided that I would try my best to keep my cool even if I don't like what's said to me.

"You can call me Alya. Have a seat." I caught myself staring at Alya and quickly put my head down. She was beautiful wearing a cream pants suit and matching heels. Her short platinum blonde hair complimented her caramel-colored skin. It was something about her that made the nervousness that dwelled in the pit of my stomach five minutes ago, subside. I felt at ease and couldn't put my finger on why.

"Thank you. I got your message about you having some information that may help me with my unemployment claim."

"Yes, but before we get into that. Tell me a little about yourself and your goals. This is my first year at this office, and in this type of role and I want to make sure I take the time to get to know all the people who come to my office. It helps me to see how I can better serve you."

"Well, I've wanted to be a nurse all my life. I remember my GiGi used to watch old episodes of this really old TV show named *Julia* with Diahann Carroll. I used to think she was so pretty. Watching her play a nurse and the fact that my GiGi always wanted to be one as well made me want to be a nurse, too. I know I'm kinda old to be in school trying to pursue this, but I didn't go to college as soon as I finished high school. I decided to take a bit of a break to get myself together," I gently shook my leg as I started to chew on my bottom lip again.

"That sounds awesome. I love the nursing profession myself. I have never been a nurse, but I have several people close to me who are in the profession. You must be a special person because it truly takes special people to care for others in the way that nurses do. You have to have a lot of love, care, and compassion in your heart."

"I agree. I'd like to think that my GiGi is responsible for instilling that into me at a young age. She was never able to pursue her dream of becoming a nurse, so in some way, I feel like she gets to live that dream through me. I can't enroll right now because I owe some money. That's why the unemployment benefits will be helpful to me until I get steady work. The last thing I want to do is let my GiGi down. So, what are the options you have for me? Am I gonna be able to get the benefits?"

"So, unfortunately, we still can't approve you for benefits. But, I wanted to share some information about a program we have that may be beneficial to you. It's in a home for people dealing with substance abuse and other mental health issues. Basically, you would be there to help the doctors and nurses who come in to do checks and distribute medications. It's run by my church."

"Sounds interesting. What made you think this would be a

good fit for me? I'm just curious." I hoped she wasn't trying to be funny by putting me in a situation to be around other people considered crazy by most. I didn't need any reminders of anything I was trying to forget.

"Well your prior work history, of course. You already have experience being a nursing assistant, so I thought this might work for you."

"Ms. Thom-"

"Alya."

"Alya, I mean this in the humblest way possible, but I can't see myself working in a spot like that. There are things that I don't choose to share that prevent me from being able to do that."

"What other options do you have? The pay is more than what you made at your last job," she asked.

"Not many, but I will try to come up with something. I just can't work in that type of environment. I hope you understand where I'm coming from."

"Well, I'll tell you what. Just go home and think about it. I'll give you a few days, then I'll have my assistant reach out to you."

"Ok. I don't want to seem unappreciative. I really am thankful for you reaching out to me, but I just have to make sure this would be a good option for me. I may be able to come up with something else to get me where I need to be."

"No problem. I'll be in touch! Now you have yourself a wonderful day," Alya said. I got up and hurried back out to Ezrail's car and hopped in.

"Why you ain't come in and say hi to that old friend you said you had that worked here?"

"Cause she was in a meeting with a girl about your size, your height, your weight, and I ain't wanna interrupt."

"Oh so your friend is Alya Thomas? How long have you known her?"

"Let's just say we go way back. Too many years for me to even remember. Feels like she's been a part of my life since I was born."

"I thought she might be your little girlfriend or something. She's gorgeous, and I know women like her have men beating her door down." I turned to see if I could read his expression, but it didn't tell me anything different from what he just said.

"Yeah, she's beautiful, but I don't see her like that."

"Oh ok. She seems real cool. I can tell she has a good heart and really wanted to help me, but her offer definitely wasn't something I wanted to take in order to make money."

"I feel you, but what else you gonna do? Do you really wanna go to nursing school?'

"Yeah, I do. I just don't want to have to wait another year or so for that to happen."

"Sometimes, you gotta realize that timing is everything."

"I guess so," I said as I turned my attention to the road. My stomach felt uneasy, but at the same time, I was starving. "You mind stopping me by the Vino's Pizza? I'm starving," I asked. I had no intention of being interrupted when I got home. All I wanted to do was get in my bed and sleep away the rest of this disastrous day.

"Yeah, I got you, but I need to make two stops real quick. They'll be fast, I promise." I shrugged my shoulders. It wasn't like this was my ride, and it wasn't like I had anything else to do at the moment.

Ezrail pulled up to the Discount Tire shop. "What are we doing here? I told you not to worry about it. My fiancé will take care of it when he gets back."

"Nah, Ma. You can't be out here with no ride. Seems like your fiancé been gone for a minute. When he coming back anyway?" Ezrail stared at me as if he was looking through my soul. It felt like he could read my thoughts and insecurities.

"Damn– I mean, he'll be back soon."

"Look, just let me get this tire for you. I got sisters, and I would never want them to be out back. Just look at it as me paying it forward so if one of my sisters need help one day, I already put that in the atmosphere for them to receive it." Ezrail didn't say another word. He got out and headed in the tire shop. It only took him about ten minutes before he returned with the store clerk in tow carrying the tire. They placed it in the trunk, and we were on our way again.

We were in the car for another fifteen minutes before we pulled up on a remote street to what looked like an abandoned green warehouse.

"If I didn't know any better, I'd think this would be a place I needed to stay far away from," I commented.

"Like I told you before, I'm not here to take your life, but chill for a minute. I'll be back." Ezrail disappeared behind the heavy steel door of the warehouse. About five minutes later, he emerged carrying a blue cooler and a brown paper bag. He popped the trunk and placed the cooler inside. Before he could get inside the car, a short, white woman with a black pixie cut wearing an ankle-length black trench coat approached him and handed him another brown bag. They exchanged words before she disappeared behind the steel door.

"So, I lied to you. I wasn't expecting the package that I received, and I gotta put it in the next person's hands before I drop you off. I promise this is my last stop, before I take you to Vino's."

"It's all good. I ain't got shit else to do at the moment," I responded. Ezrail opened the two brown paper bags and pulled out more money than I had ever laid my eyes on at one time. I tried to keep my attention on what was going on outside of the car and not the money that sat in his lap. After he separated some of the money, he slid the rest under his car seat and pulled off to head to the next destination.

Our next stop was in a nice Buckhead neighborhood that featured restored craftsman-style houses. We pulled up in the driveway of a blue house with a huge wrap-around porch complete with a swing. The yard was neatly manicured. It was the type of home I dreamed of raising me and Lucky's children in.

Ezrail pulled his phone out and sent a text to the person I assume he was here to see. A short white man dressed in black scrubs could be seen from the picture window in the front of the house. He came to the door and Ezrail stepped out and grabbed the cooler from the car. After handing the cooler and a wad of cash to the man, Ezrail wrapped up his conversation and got back in the car.

"Aight, let's get you to Vino's and back home." As we pulled out the driveway, the man Ezrail came to see hopped in his SUV and pulled out behind us. He eventually turned down another street as we headed in the direction of our apartment complex.

"So what exactly do you do again?" I asked, breaking the silence between us.

"Let's just say I'm in the business of changing lives. I help people in a multitude of ways to realize their true potential. Once I do that, that helps me build my team and then we continue to the mission to change lives.'

"Change lives? Change lives how? I damn sure need some things in my life to change."

"Ma, when you're ready to embrace all of you, even the parts you hide, you'll be able to change your life."

Chapter Twelve
Autumn

The coldness of the tile floor made my knees ache as I held my head over the toilet bowl. It was the third time in three hours that I'd been in this position, forcefully depositing the contents of my stomach into this porcelain bowl. I was surprised there was anything else left in my stomach. It seemed I had thrown up everything in me except my organs.

I needed to take a pregnancy test, but I had no energy to leave the house at the moment. As much as I hated to call Tamela and put her in my business, there was no one else I felt comfortable enough with calling to bring me a test.

"Hey, bitch, you busy?" I asked when Tam answered the phone.

"Not really. I just stopped at Kroger to grab me some ice cream so I can go home and watch some movies. What's up with you?" Tam asked.

"Well, since you asked, and since you're already at the store, can you grab me a pregnancy test and drop it off here?"

"Wait. What? Not you thinking you're pregnant! This is something you've always wanted!" Tam squealed with delight.

"Yeah, but not like this. I didn't plan on being a single parent," I said with sadness in my voice.

"I get it, but at this point you can only do one of two things if you are pregnant. And that's have an abortion or have the baby. That's a decision you'll have to make though."

"True, but let me at least see if I'm pregnant first. Get me the test. I'll CashApp you the money for it."

"Girl, keep your lil money. You already know you can't afford to pay for the test."

"Damn, you ain't gotta keep reminding me that I'm broke!" I smacked my mouth and sucked my teeth. If Tam was in my presence right now, she'd know she was pissing me off.

"Whatever, girl. I'll see you in twenty," Tam said.

I tossed my phone on the bed and laid across it. I was exhausted. I was averaging about four hours of sleep every night. No matter how hard I tried to rest, I just couldn't. Now, the sickness was taking over and causing even more issues with my sleep pattern.

The light tapping at my front door interrupted my thoughts. Twenty minutes went by faster than I anticipated, and now Tam was waiting for me to let her in. Easing out of the bed, I slid my slippers on and headed to the door.

"Damn, it took you long enough to open the door," Tam said.

"First of all, a hello would have been nice. Second, calm your ass down," I responded.

"Whatever! I see you still ain't cleaned this nasty ass apartment up," Tam stated.

"Girl, just give me the damn test." Tamela retrieved the test from her purse and handed it to me. I left her standing there and headed to the bathroom to take the test. Closing the door behind me, I leaned against the door and sucked in air. Maybe having this baby would be the thing that would bring me and Lucky back together. While looking down at my engagement ring, my hope in becoming Lucky's wife was somewhat restored.

"You'll never have his heart. I told you this from day one, but what did you do? You ignored me. That baby ain't gone make him come back to you. One day you gone learn to listen to me."

"Shit! Let me hurry up." I opened the test and slid my panties down and peed on the stick. The anxiousness I felt was starting to make me feel like I had to throw up once again. I splashed some cold water on my face to try and help the feeling to subside.

"Autumn, what the hell is taking you so long? I'm gonna have your whole house cleaned up before you get out here with them results!" Tamela yelled.

"Give me a sec. And nobody asked you to clean up shit." The timer I set on my phone chimed. Taking in a deep breath as I looked down to read the results, I tried to compose myself.

Not Pregnant.

The test betrayed me. I really thought I was pregnant. I hadn't been too good with tracking my periods lately, so I couldn't remember the last time I had one. Although I didn't have a huge baby bump, there was a little bulge that was making my pants fit tighter around my waist. And the constant morning sickness. So many emotions flowed through me. I was disappointed and sad, but at the same time I was relieved to not be bringing a baby into the world without being married. I was in no state to be concerned about a baby right now.

"I'm not pregnant," I said as I exited the bathroom. Tamela was in the kitchen with a broom in hand sweeping up all the trash that was on the floor.

"You good? You ok with that?" she asked.

"I don't have a choice but to be ok with it. What else can I do? It's probably for the best anyway. I can barely take care of myself let alone a child," I admitted.

"Are you ok, Autumn? You know you can be real with me. I ain't here to judge because Lord knows I have my issues. I can just tell that shit ain't right with you. I heard you in the bathroom."

"You heard what?" I quizzed. I don't know what she thought she heard, but I know she didn't hear shit from me.

"So you just gone act like you weren't in the bathroom talking to yourself in funny voices?"

"Damn, I didn't think it was a crime to talk to yourself," I quipped.

"It ain't, but when you start doing voices and shit, I gotta question some shit. Look, I know that mental illness shit is in your family. If you are suffering, you gotta get help. The more you avoid taking care of your mind, the more you're setting yourself up for failure. Health is wealth and that includes your mental health, too."

"I'm fine," I lied. It was true. I could finally admit that I was talking to myself at times.

"Well, just know I'm here for you if you need me. Matter of

fact, why don't you go on in your room and lay down. You look like you could use some rest anyway. I'm gonna clean up out here so you can at least have a clean kitchen and living room. All of this clutter and chaos you've surrounded yourself with is just a manifestation of what's really going on in your mind."

"You know what, I'm going to take you up on your offer to go lay my ass down. I am exhausted. I just hope that I'm able to fall asleep."

"Let me make you some chamomile tea. That should help relax you. Go ahead in your room and lay down. I'll bring it to you."

Before I reached my room, I glanced out the window to see Ezrail getting in his car. He was dressed in all black and looked like Morpheus from *The Matrix*. A more stylish version, though.

I pushed all of the books, food wrappers, and bowls off my bed and got in under my fluffy white down blanket that was now dingy and stank. Tam walked in handing me a mug with the tea.

"How can you really get any rest in here with all this shit everywhere? No wonder why you can't get any sleep. I can't sleep in a dirty room. I know I love the fuck out of you, because I'm prepared to spend the rest of my day off cleaning this atrocious apartment. Queens don't live like the pigs, Autumn."

"I thought you said you wasn't here to judge me, yet here you are judging me. I know this shit is out of control. I just don't have the energy to clean it up right now. And I appreciate you helping me, but please stop judging me. I've had enough of that to last me a lifetime." I admitted.

"I'm sorry, sis. Let me at least change your bedding right

now. Sit over there in that chair while I strip your bed. Where's the clean linen?"

"It's some in the hall closet," I said as I got up and sat on the gray chair by my bedroom window. Tamela quickly changed my sheets and I got back in bed. She went to the kitchen and returned with a mug in her hand. The tea seemed like it was giving what it was supposed to give, and I drifted off into a deep sleep. When I woke up, my apartment was spotless. Tam was gone, but she left a hundred-dollar bill on my coffee table for me to pay my light bill because she found the disconnect notice when she was cleaning up.

I looked around my apartment and at the note Tam left me as tears spilled from eyes and wet the paper. It was a reminder that I was spiraling out of control. Everything in my life reflected the path I was now on. If I didn't get help soon, I didn't know what might go wrong in my life next. I wanted to tell Tamela, but I wasn't ready, yet. It made me happy to know that when the time came, she'd be there for me no matter what. She'd always been a solid friend to me, and I was thankful for that.

Chapter Thirteen
Autumn

"I want in," I said as Ezrail stood in his doorway with a bewildered look on his face. He scratched his head and leaned against his door. I peeped inside his apartment, which was drastically different from mine. Ezrail's apartment was neat and clean with only the simple necessities. He moved back to invite me into his space, and I happily entered. I shuddered at the coolness of the air that hit me when I entered his place.

"Why is it so cold in here?" I inquired.

"Hello to you, too, Ma," Ezrail said. He pulled out a wood, steel legged bar stool and took a seat and offered me one as well. "What exactly is it that you want into?"

"Whatever it is that you're doing to make them bands I saw you with the other day, that's what I want to do."

"Let me ask you something. Are you able to fully handle the fact that there's a part of you that most won't accept, but has the ability to put you in position to have some of the things you want now?"

"What's this part of me that you keep referring to? Why you think you have so much figured out about me? You don't even know me for real."

"I told you, I know your type. I know you hear voices. You've spent your whole life running from the thing that makes you like someone close to you. I know this because what you have is mostly genetic. Most see it as a curse. But not me. I see it as a gift. You just have to learn how to use it to your advantage."

"Use it to my advantage how? Hearing voices and trying not to act on the shit they tell me to do ain't hardly a gift. I got into a fight and all the voice wanted me to do was kill the motherfuckers who were aggravating me."

"Ok. So, check this out. What if I told you that you no longer had to suppress those desires?"

"What are you saying right now, Ezrail? Like, I really need you to be crystal clear."

"You allow the voices to act out their desires, and we both get what we want from it."

"Again, you're beating around the bush. What do you mean act out their desires? My voice tells me to harm people. Even kill them."

"That's perfect. Let them kill, then."

I got up from my seat. Clearly, Ezrail had lost his mind if he thought I was going to go out and become a murderer. "Are you out of your rabbit ass mind? I can't go around killing people for sport."

"Listen, Ma, it's not for sport. It's for a higher cause. One bigger than us. And you asked for this." Ezrails gaze. The fact that he so casually suggested I started murdering people didn't sit well with me either.

"So let me get this straight. You expect me to commit murder for a higher cause? What the fuck is the higher cause because I'm truly not understanding you right now."

"Girl, if you know like I know, you'd take the offer. Let me have my time to shine. I already told you that you were doomed anyway."

"I don't expect you to do anything you don't want to do, but the fact that you're still here in the living room of my apartment tells me that what I said has piqued your interest. What's holding you back? This lifestyle is already a part of you. It's already embedded in your DNA. No need to keep fighting, Ma. Set yourself free. You won't regret it."

"It's already in my DNA? What makes you think you know so much about me and you still didn't answer my question. What the fuck is the higher cause?"

"First, The Elite One sent me here. Most would call him Satan or the devil, but I prefer the Elite One. The same things most people turn to God for, he can also supply. His timeline is much quicker. He's the reason I know so much about you and how that brain of yours works. The Elite One gives me the source of knowledge to know things about people. I knew you when I saw you the very first time. I knew all of the things I needed to know about you to know that you would be perfect for this mission.

"Mission? So, killing people is now a mission?"

"For me, yes. I like to look at myself as a collector. I have a team of unique individuals in place who help me complete the mission. These are the people who would be considered misfits in most circles if people knew their secrets, but not with me. They help me get the thing I need."

"Ezrail, one thing I liked about you when I first met you was that you seemed like a straight shooter. Right now, you're irritating the fuck out of me with all this beating around the bush."

"But you just said you wasn't interested, Ma. Why does how long I take to get to the point really matter to you unless – like I said earlier – you're interested in my proposition?"

"Whatever. Let me leave because I ain't interested in committing murder. All I want is to get my money up and get my life back on track. I'm not signing up to become a murderer."

"You can walk right out of here right now with all the bull-shit problems you got in your life and go holla at my girl, Alya. I think she may have an offer that will better suit you. However, if shit don't work out the way you want it to, I'll be here, but my offer is only for a short amount of time."

I headed out the door without saying another word to Ezrail. There was nothing left to talk about. This nigga really wanted me to commit murder. So many thoughts ran through my mind. What would happen if I got caught? What if I liked it?

Chapter Fourteen
Autumn

I t had been four months since everything that was normal for me changed and caused my life to crash down around me. I sat on my couch and thought about the situation I was currently in. There wasn't a thing that had worked in my favor lately. Getting fired, losing my man, and knowing I couldn't help GiGi like I wanted to had me in a fucked up predicament. All of my dreams had been stripped from me in the blink of an eye.

Between the time I was in Ezrails apartment and now, the leasing agent had been to my apartment. She let her presence be known by the piece of paper she taped on my door. My heart rate sped up because I already knew what it was. I snatched the notice off the door to see the word 'Eviction' spread across it in large red letters.

"See, shit just keeps getting worse for you. It's not like you would be alone to do what Ezrail asked. It's not you who would be doing shit! It would be us!"

"Damn! Why won't you just leave me the fuck alone?"

There wasn't shit I wanted to do more right now than to blow my brains out, but I didn't want to hurt my GiGi. I never wanted to do anything to bring her more of the pain that her entire life had been filled with.

There was no way I could do what Ezrail suggested, so I decided that taking Alya up on her offer was the best thing for me to do to try to get my life back on track. I went to my bedroom to lay down. Exhaustion from not getting enough sleep was taking its toll on me. I slid my jeans off, threw them on the floor, and got in my bed with my phone in hand. I could feel crumbs from the potato chips I ate earlier sticking to my skin, but I didn't care. I sent Alya a text.

Me, 7:01 pm to Alya: *Hi Alya. I've been thinking about your offer. I am willing to give it a shot. At this point I'm desperate. I could use the income right now. Please let me know when I can start.*

Thoughts of Lucky invaded my mind. I missed him so much. I twirled my engagement ring on my finger and became teary eyed. He really left me for that Sponge Bob-shaped bitch, Whitney. It took all of me not to hop in my car and drive by her house. I knew Lucky was there, but me popping up over there wasn't going to solve anything.

My phone chimed, and I knew it was Alya responding to me. She let me know I could start immediately. I was thankful because I needed to get some money coming in. It wasn't like I had too many other options. The eviction notice I received earlier solidified that fact.

* * *

THE BRIGHTNESS OF THE MORNING SUN DANCED ON MY chocolate skin as I rode down the highway to the address Alya sent me by text. Traffic was heavy as expected, so I called Alya to alert her to my possible tardiness. She let me know that it wouldn't be a problem.

Immediately upon entering the group home, I wanted to leave. "Oh, nah. I can't do this," I whispered to myself.

"Ms. Carrington?" a voice called out to me. I turned around to an older black gentleman who easily stood over six feet tall. He had white hair, light skin, and the same eyes that Alya had.

"Uh, yes, that's me," I reluctantly replied.

"I'm Pastor Thomas. We are so pleased to have you here. My daughter, Alya, told me so much about you and your background. She says you want to be a nurse?"

"Yes, I do. I have about a year left before that dream will be a reality for me. You said Alya was your daughter? She didn't mention that to me."

"I see. Yes, she's my daughter. Let me show you around." Pastor Thomas led me through the home. "This particular house serves women. A lot of the ladies here are moms, and due to some traumatic events in their lives, turned to drugs to cope. We try to re-integrate them into society. You may see some of them going through withdrawals. They may even become violent at times. Don't let that scare you." I passed a room where a woman lay out on the bed looking like a zombie. The sight of her nearly knocked the wind out of me because seeing her like that reminded me of Winter and what I might become.

"We finally found our tribe."

"No the hell we haven't!" I bellowed.

"Excuse me?"

"Oh, uh, nothing," I responded.

"Here is the office you'll be working out of," Pastor Thomas said as he led me into a small room. "You can leave your things here and then I'd like you to join me in the community living space. Several of the women will be participating in a group discussion. We do this every morning."

"Ok," I said, smiling weakly. I placed my purse in the drawer and headed down the hallway. As I approached the living area a short, white woman with long blond hair approached me.

"You new here? What's wrong with you? Let me guess. You're manic aren't ya?"

"I'm not here for treatment," I replied as I rolled my eyes at her.

"You should be. I can tell by them eyes, that you ain't right in the head!"

"Linda! Leave Ms. Carrington alone! She works here. Now come on in here and get settled before the group starts," Pastor Thomas chastised. Linda looked back at me, raised two fingers to her eyes then pointed them back at me. I tried to act like I didn't see her as I walked around her and took a seat.

An older woman with mocha brown skin took a seat in the middle of the circle the other women formed. She had the same eyes as Alya, so I figured it may have been her mother.

"Good Morning, ladies. We have a few new ladies here this morning as well as new staff," she said as she looked in my direction. There was a warmness her presence brought that slightly made me feel a little more comfortable. "I'm Lady

Thomas, Pastor Thomas's wife, and I'll be leading the group today. I want to give out new ladies an opportunity to introduce themselves and tell us what they wish to achieve while here." Lady Thomas chose the first woman to give her story.

I looked around the room at the many faces that were there. Women old, young, Black, white, and Hispanic filled the room. They shared their stories of substance abuse and mental anguish. Listening to them recount so many horrible details of their life weighed heavily on me.

"You should have taken Ezrail's offer. This shit right here ain't it," Kalidah said.

I chewed on my bottom lip until I tasted blood as I listened to each of the woman that shared. Two of the women had similar stories to mine and before I knew it, tears were falling from my eyes as I heard the pain in their voices. It was too much for me.

I left the living area and returned to my office, shutting the door behind me. I tried to get myself together, but I knew there was no way I could go back out there. Working here would be too hard for me and a painful reminder of all the things I needed to forget. A soft tap at the door interrupted my thoughts.

"Autumn? You in here?" Pastor Thomas asked. I opened the door to let him in. "You okay? I know what you heard may have been overwhelming." I took that as my que to let him know this wasn't going to work for me. Tossing my purse on my shoulder, I prepared to leave.

"Pastor Thomas, I don't think I can work here. Alya didn't know but being in a place like this is triggering for me. I just can't stay here. Thank you so much for the opportunity, but I just can't do it." I hurried through the door to the front of the house ignoring Pastor Thomas's words as he trailed behind me. I quickly exited the house. I knew as soon as Alya suggested this opportunity, it wasn't for me.

As soon as I got in my car and pulled off, my phone started ringing. Immediately I knew it was Alya so I sent her to voicemail. I wasn't explaining my decision to her. She put me in a place where I was surrounded by the very things I wanted nothing to do with. She wouldn't let up on the phone calls, so I reluctantly answered after her seventh try.

"Ms. Thomas, I'm not going back," I told her.

"Autumn, I knew it would be difficult for you to be there. But, I wanted you to find hope there. I think you should consider going back."

"Nah, I'm good. You won't catch me going back. I don't need to be reminded of my mother every chance I get. I'm trying to forget as much about her as I can."

"You're trying to forget her or are you trying to forget the hard things about yourself?"

"What's that supposed to mean?"

"Autumn, I know more about you than you may know. I know everything you're dealing with, and I wanted you to see that you can overcome the very things that you're trying to run from."

"What things are those since you think you know so much about me? You been talking to Ezrail about me?"

"Yes, we've talked about you, but he didn't tell me anything I didn't already know about you. You see, Ezrail has his way of doing things and I have mine. I just want to help you, Autumn.

My intentions towards you are good. Ezrail has other plans for you."

"Help me how? My whole life I've prayed to not be like my mama, yet here I am following in her footsteps."

"You don't have to keep it going though. God has heard you, but you're still holding on by trying to do things your way. If you come back to the group home, I can make sure you get the help you need."

"I told you God doesn't hear you. Look at your life. It's clear. Hang up on her and stop wasting our time. Ezrail's proposition is the only way."

"I'm sorry, Alya. God doesn't hear me, and I ain't going back to work at the group home."

"I can't do anything but respect your decision, just know, I'm here if you need me. Oh, and God does hear you. He'll always have a place for you. You just have to be open to receiving all that he has for you."

We ended the call. There was no way I'd be going back so there was nothing else for me to do except call Ezrail and move forward. Maybe Kalidah would stop taunting me if she finally got her way. She was getting harder to control, and I was getting tired of trying to hide her anyway.

Chapter Fifteen
Autumn

"Ezrail, I've been thinking long and hard about your proposition. At this point, my life has become about survival and at the rate I'm going, I may be dead sooner rather than later," I said as I sat down. "Tell me what I gotta do."

Ezrail sat on his couch staring at me. He pulled hard on the blunt he was smoking, but remained silent. I lightly tapped my foot against the floor and started chewing on my bottom lip as I anticipated his words.

"You sure you want to do this? There's a lot that comes with this situation. This ain't some job you can just quit when you feel like it," he said.

I readjusted myself in my seat and swallowed the lump that had formed in my throat before I spoke. "Yes, I'm aware," I replied.

"The first thing I need you to do is tell me about the voices."

"We back to that again?"

"Yeah, it's an integral part of why I wanted you on the team anyway. I need to know more."

"Well, her name is Kalidah. She gives me the courage to say and do things I wouldn't ordinarily do. Been part of my life since I was about five or six. And trying to protect me since."

"Protect you? How does she do that?" The intensity in his stare increased.

"She's been trying to take over for a while, but I never let her. She wants to do things I would never do. Hurt people. Sometimes even kill them. But I can't let her." A single tear filled my left eye and rolled down my cheek. The ache in my heart caused my throat to constrict. Visions from my past filled my mind. A secret I'd been keeping for years haunted my memories.

"See the problem with you, Ma, is that you've been letting fear hold you back. I've watched you for quite some time. I've always seen your potential, but the problem is you didn't. You avoid the thing that makes you, you. And, you think your dream life isn't obtainable unless you hide your true self. But the life you desire won't be yours until you embrace every aspect of who you are. I'm here to help you get there faster."

"And exactly how is that? I've asked you this question multiple times, and it seems you're trying to evade the answer." I nervously chewed my bottom lip and took a seat on the couch next to him. Ezrail's evasiveness added to my already mounting anxiety.

"It's simple. I need organs, but more importantly, souls. When y'all kill, it helps me get what I need for the Elite One. Harvesting the organs helps the team. Organs from strong, healthy men sell for top dollar. Right now, you need money. What's that the Bible says? *'Money answereth all things.'* We can help each other get to the bag."

"I don't know nothing about a Bible verse, but I'm trying to make sure I'm tracking what you're saying. So, you're telling me you want me to commit murder? You must have lost your rabbit ass mind. I need money, but I aint' trying to catch a case in the process of getting to a damn bag. And you need souls? What the hell does that even mean?"

"It ain't like you ain't done it before. I know your secrets."

"I don't know what you're talking about." I got up and walked to the door.

"You know exactly what I'm talking about. Kalidah's first kill was someone who hurt you. Right after that happened is when you were placed on medication to suppress Kalidah, but you didn't like the way the medicine made you feel so you stopped taking it once you got older. As a result of that, you've been trying to live with Kalidah, but she's dying to get out. It's like she watches from the shadows. Waiting for you to let her be free. There ain't much you're going to be able to do soon. You got two choices. Embrace it and get this bag or keep doing what you doing and see how far you get."

"Don't walk out that door. I'm tired of hiding in your shadows. It's my time, and you ain't gonna take that from me," Kalidah challenged.

I sat back down. I needed more understanding. Making fast money would be the solution to a lot of problems I currently have. GiGi needed my help, and I needed to be able to keep a roof over our head.

"I thought you'd see things my way. Now let's get down to

the particulars. Your beauty is a weapon. Use it wisely. Allow Kalidah to protect and avenge you when she wants to. Let her take over. She'll know who and when." He got up from his seat and headed to the kitchen.

"Finally, somebody sees things my way."

"And just how do you plan to keep me from getting caught?"

"There's a team of us. Here, take this," Ezrail said, handing me a cell phone he retrieved from a drawer in the kitchen. "When you're done doing what I need you to, call me and the team, and we will take it from there. Oh, and your cut of the money will be fifteen thousand per job."

"How often is this supposed to happen?"

"As often as Kalidah desires. Remember, she's the driver now. You're in the passenger seat enjoying the ride."

"There's already someone I have in mind," Kalidah uttered.

"Bet. Set it up and send me the details," Ezrail responded. A look of pure amusement spread across his face.

"Say less," Kalidah growled. Her voice was deep, but confident.

I WRESTLED WITH THE THOUGHT OF KALIDAH TAKING over. Mainly because I knew I would be losing control of myself in the process, and what she was capable of always scared me. Thoughts of the time when I had no control over her flooded my mind.

I was around twelve years old when Kalidah fully manifested herself in my life. She'd been there for a while, but she never fully took over and did things that scared me. She was my imaginary friend at first. Later, she became my protector. She hated seeing me in pain.

I could hear the voice of my tormentor ringing in my head. Tenisha Harris hated me. She'd been picking on me for what seemed like forever, although it was only for a period of about six months. Still, six months is a long time to have to deal with someone bullying you. I wasn't real clear on the reason she even started messing with me. I tried to stay quiet and to myself for the most part. Maybe that was the reason. The last time she ever had the audacity to come for me flashed through my mind.

It seemed like Tenisha towered over me as we stood in the bathroom of my middle school. But, in reality she and I were about the same size. It was the fear that she evoked in me that made her seem bigger than what she was. The sound of my teeth knocking against each other and my lips vibrating emboldened Tenisha. As she got close to me, the sour stench of her breath nearly caused me to gag.

"You think you so cute with all that long hair and shit! You ain't better than me or anybody else in this school!" Tenisha screamed. Her friends, Tiffany and Candice stood around laughing and hyping Tenisha up.

"She ain't even all that! Look at them shoes she got on? Who the fuck where's them Keds anyway?" Tiffany asked. She stood there staring at me looking like a peacock with her huge eyes and three-inch fanned ponytail sitting on top of her head.

"Tenisha, listen, I don't think I'm better than anybody," I said, my voice cracking with fear. I tried to move away from her, but she pushed me so hard I fell on the nasty bathroom floor. I hurried to get up off the floor and regain my composure.

"*Shut up with your weak ass! I knew you wasn't gonna do shit to me! You too cute to fight,*" Tenisha bellowed. Tears streamed down my face as I tried to find my voice. Tenisha took my show of weakness as a sign to continue what she had started. She wound her fist up and hit me with a left hook that sent me crashing into the bathroom sink. That's when I heard Kalidah's voice come through my mouth for the first time.

"*Get the fuck off of her!*" Kalidah screamed! Her voice was heavier than my soft, squeaky voice and boomed as it bounced off the bathroom walls. Tenisha's mouth gaped, and her already huge eyes bulged out of her head. Clearly, she'd never prepared for the possibility that she might actually get her ass kicked.

A surge of adrenaline coursed through my body as Kalidah took over me. Kalidah immediately started landing blow after blow to Tenisha's head. She grabbed hold of the three inches of hair she had and forced her to the ground. Tiffany tried to jump in, but Kalidah let up off her just long enough to smash her head into the sink. Crystal ran to try to get help.

"*Talk your shit now! You was big and bad a few minutes ago! Keep talking now, bitch!*" I took in everything that was happening but could do nothing to stop the progression of what happened next. Once Tenisha was on the ground, Kalidah kicked her multiple times in her face and head. Blood leaked from her mouth.

"*Please, stop! I'm sorry! Please!*" Tenisha groveled, but Kalidah wasn't trying to hear that. I wanted to stop Kalidah, but she was too far gone. "*Autumn...Autumn.*" Tenisha's voice was barely above a whisper.

"*Nah, don't beg now! You thought you could put your hands on Autumn and get away with that shit!*" Kalidah screamed. She *was completely oblivious to the school resource officer who entered the bathroom, but I heard the commotion as he entered the bathroom. By then, Tenisha was balled up on the floor with her knees pulled into her chest. She barely moved while Kalidah continued to pummel her with her fists and feet.*

The resource officer rushed Kalidah and pulled her away from Tenisha's body. "Stop! Autumn, calm down!" Officer North yelled. "Somebody get the nurse! She's hurt pretty bad in here. This doesn't look good."

Thinking about how angry Kalidah got made my heart and mind race. After the incident in the bathroom at school, my grandmother had me evaluated and that's when I was diagnosed with dissociative identity disorder and manic depression. From that point on, I was on medication to control Kalidah. As I got older, I felt like I had control over Kalidah, so I stopped taking them. As long as Lucky and I were together, he never got a glimpse of her. No one close to me did. Only my family could tell when Kalidah was trying to show herself.

Up until now, I never even wanted to acknowledge that this was my reality. I worked really hard to try and hide the reality of who I was. Even though I had plenty of beauty, I felt like a monster on the inside. The same monster that I saw when I looked at my mother was hiding in me.

Part of me now felt relieved. I was tired of trying to quiet her voice. It was freeing to in a sense to finally succumb to her presence. Finally, she'd do things I've been too afraid to do. The urges I tried to suppress, I didn't have to anymore thanks to Ezrail pushing me to embrace the thing I'd been running from.

Chapter Sixteen
Autumn

One week had passed since I took Ezrail up on his offer, and here I was getting ready to do the one thing I never thought I could. Kalidah made it really easy for me to agree to being in this time and place with the man I'd loved for the last two years. As much as I loved Lucky, bitterness also resided in my heart when it came to him.

It was easier than I thought to get Lucky to agree to meet with me. I lied and told him that a check had come in the mail for him from one of his tenants. He wasn't gonna miss out on any money, so he agreed to have me meet him at his new place along with letting me know that he missed me. If he missed me so much, he would have come home, but he didn't. The truth of the matter was he just missed what was between my legs.

I looked back at him as I threw my ass back. There was a fierce intensity in his eyes. There was no denying that he was enjoying the way I winded my ass on his dick. My pussy was dripping wet with satisfaction. My adrenaline was on a thousand, but not because I was turned on. It had been a while since our last encounter together.

My mind raced back to the last time I saw Lucky. He was looking all happy and in love with that bitch he was with. The hurt of seeing him with her never left me. He had been my entire world for two long years. I poured my blood, sweat, and tears into our relationship. I was determined to put in the work required to make our relationship a success, but we weren't on the same page when it came to that. I remember feeling the sting that his words left in my heart. It took me a long time to recover from the deep well of sadness he left me in. His words hit me like flying daggers piercing my heart and penetrating my soul. They were forever embedded in my memory.

"Autumn, this shit is dead. I can't do this anymore," Lucky said, *brazenly.*

"Don't start that bullshit. Now you want to act like I'm the problem when the whole time you been cheating?" I asked.

"You're just not someone I feel I can build with. I am tired of trying to force something that just ain't meant to be. We should have just stayed fuck buddies instead of trying to take shit further," He coldly replied.

By this time, my heart was beating out of my chest. I couldn't believe what I was hearing him say. I accepted everything that came with him, but the sentiment was not reciprocated. I had long felt like I wasn't good enough or what Lucky wanted. I tried to be like the other bitch I knew he consistently messed around on me with, but I couldn't measure. The only thing that pretty much kept Lucky coming back was my cold head game and good pussy. Hence, the reason why he was here with me tonight. Even after leaving me for that hyena looking bitch months ago, he still couldn't find another woman who could do it like me. I planned to take advantage of the fact that he wanted my pussy tonight.

"You like when I wind it like that, baby?" I asked him. Kalidah took a backseat and let me handle things until we were ready to move forward. Having her with me gave me the confidence I needed to get through the night.

"Damn right! I missed this pussy!" Lucky panted.

"Let me get on top and show you what else you've been missing. Lay down," I stated as I moved so Lucky could position himself on the bed. Before mounting him, I took dick in my mouth and slurped the sweetness of my own juices. I peered up at him as his eyes rolled back in his head. I had him right where I wanted him to be. Drunk off the sex. I climbed on top and slid his dick inside my slick pussy. I began to rock my hips back and forth. The feeling of him being inside me took me back. I used to crave his dick.

"Feel good, baby?" I whispered.

"Hell yeah," Lucky replied.

"Look at me, baby" I commanded. Lucky did as I told him to. I slowly started to speed up the tempo as I continued riding his dick. I stared into his eyes as they roamed my body and settled on my stomach. I searched them to see if I could detect a hint of love for me. There was none, though and I felt it when I connected with his hazel eyes.

"Yo, what's up with your stomach? You pregnant?" Lucky asked.

"No, baby. I just gained weight."

"You sure?"

"Why are we talking about this? I took a test, and it was negative."

"Shit...This pussy definitely feels like pregnant pussy. Shit feels amazing."

"Tell me how you like it, baby," I whispered.

"Autumn, you know I love the pussy," he admitted.

"Is that right? Keep telling me how much you love it," I responded as I began to quicken the pace on his dick. I leaned forward to kiss his full lips. I stayed in that position.

"Autumn, this shit feels so good. I'm about to cum," Lucky whispered. His toes curled as gripped my ass and plunged deeper inside of me. Lucky looked at me again and I was reminded of the love that wasn't there, only the lust. As he climaxed, I slid the knife from underneath my pillow and sliced his neck. He never saw it coming. Blood flowed from his neck like a fountain. He grabbed his neck with both of his hands. I could hear him gurgling as he struggled to breathe. I sat on top of him with his dick still inside of me and watched him struggle to live. A smile spread across my face.

"This is how she felt the day you left her. She struggled to breathe. Now you know exactly how she felt, nigga! Seems like today you ain't so lucky, Lucky," Kalidah said as she took over. I watched his life leave his eyes and I felt an overwhelming sense of both sadness and satisfaction. I peered down at his lifeless body, then spat in his face and got up off of him to clean myself. I picked up the phone and called Ezrail. Killing Lucky was easier than I thought it would be. I was doubly rewarded with revenge and money.

"Come up. The door is unlocked. I know you have to move fast to get what you need," I stated as I hung up.

I walked in the bathroom of Lucky's small apartment and looked at myself. I laughed as I looked at my blood-streaked face. I finally felt like I had taken my power back. This nigga pretty much left me for dead, and now the tables had turned. As life left his body, I felt rejuvenated. I was in a dark hole the last three months trying to pick up the pieces of my life after he walked out the door. He had the audacity to come only because he wanted some ass. Well, that call cost him, just like him wasting two years of my life cost me.

"I hope the booty call was worth it," I mumbled to myself. I heard Ezrail open the door and enter the apartment.

"Autumn, where you at?" he asked.

"I'm in the bathroom," I revealed as I slipped into my satin chemise so that I could help Ezrail complete what we needed to do.

As I walked into the room, Ezrail had already begun doing the hard work. He had placed plastic on the floor to prepare for wrapping up Lucky's remains. . He opened the suitcase he had to remove the machete he needed to remove the organs.

"Grab the other tools in my bag. Bring the ice chests, too," Ezrail instructed. I did as he asked and watched him hack Lucky open with precision. As he removed Lucky's heart, lungs, and kidneys, I bagged them up and put them in the chest.

"The rest of the crew will be here later tonight to take care of this shit and clean up. Here," he said, handing me a paper bag with money in it. I took it out to make sure the agreed upon amount was present.

"I'm good for it. It's all there," he asserted.

"Ok. I'm still gonna check my shit, though," I expressed as I got up and put the fifteen stacks in my purse. I went back to the bathroom to wash my hands and throw on my jogging suit. I needed to leave quickly.

"You and Kalidah ready, Autumn?" Ezrail asked.

"Yep! Let's go," I said as I glanced back at Lucky's butchered body. His eyes were open. I smirked at him lying there. I felt absolutely no remorse. You do dirt, you get dirt. That's universal law and the universe just delivered Lucky exactly what he had earned.

I PULLED UP TO LUCKY'S BARBERSHOP AND SAW THE CAR I needed to see in the parking lot. It was the only one there. Kalidah convinced me that I needed to do this even though I felt like we needed to be more strategic in our approach to these killings.

I sent Ezrail a text to let him know to be prepared. I checked my makeup and adjusted the burgundy bob wig I was wearing. Getting out of the car, I adjusted the black pea coat I was wearing.

Lightly tapping on the glass door of the shop, I stood there waiting for Joe to acknowledge my presence. When he looked up and noticed it was me, a scowl appeared on his face. That didn't stop him from opening the door, though. I knew he was thirsty for me, but Kalidah was who he was getting tonight.

"The hell you want? Lucky ain't here," he said.

"I'm not here for Lucky. I came here to see you."

"Is that right?"

"Yeah," I said, running my tongue over my cherry red lips. Joe stood there staring at me to the point his saliva pooled at the side of his mouth and damn near slid down his face before he caught it.

"What you need?"

"You should know." I stepped closer and fondled his man meat through the sweatpants he wore.

"Oh, yeah?"

"Yeah, let's go back into Lucky's office," Kalidah responded. Her voice was sultry and enticing.

Joe couldn't wait to get into the office, thinking he was going to get the opportunity of a lifetime.

"I'm not sleeping with him," I said to Kalidah.

"I know. I got this. Remember what Ezrail said."

"What the fuck? Why you talking like that?"

"Shhhh," Kalidah said. "Drop your pants."

Joe quickly forgot about the question he asked and didn't waste any time doing as he was told. The smell of shit mixed with cologne suffused the room. I dropped down to my knees, but Kalidah was still in control. I began stroking his short, thick dick. His eyes rolled back in his. Although he was enjoying the moment, I wasn't. I wanted this to over as soon as possible.

"Put it in your mouth," Joe whispered.

"You want me to suck it?"

"Damn right."

Without warning, I pulled the knife I was hiding in my boot and slashed through the flesh of Joe's dick. Shock covered his face as he fell back into the chair behind him. I quickly stood to my feet and finished the job by jabbing him in the throat with my knife.

"I know you didn't really think you were getting some ass from us, you fat fuck!" Kalidah yelled as we walked out the shop.

Chapter Seventeen
Autumn

I stopped by GiGi's house to give her some of the money I made the other night. I grabbed my hoodie and put in on to hide the extra weight I was carrying. The sky was filled with heavy rain clouds ready to pour their contents at any minute. Most people hated the rain, but I loved it. It made me think of the days when I was younger. Whenever it rained, GiGi and I would spend the day baking our favorite treats and watching our favorite movies. She always tried to make my abnormal childhood somewhat normal.

I wanted to make sure GiGi was good. It hurt my heart to know that GiGi was in any type of distress over paying bills. It was her time to chill. She'd spent most of her life taking care of everyone in this family, now it was time for me to pay it forward to her.

"Hey, my baby! Come on in here and sit down," GiGi said when she saw me walk through the door. She was seated on the couch in her living room looking out the window. GiGi wore a white housecoat with pink flowers and her hair was still on sponge rollers. This wasn't like GiGi. She always made sure she was dressed, but given what she was going through, I guess she didn't have the strength to get dressed every day.

"How is everything going with the treatment plan?"

"As good as can be expected, but my God is a healer and I believe I'm gonna be better in no time. I got an appointment tomorrow, so I'm gonna catch the bus up there."

"GiGi, you're not catching a bus to your appointment. I'll take you. I'm off tomorrow anyway. I know you have been having a hard time with some of your bills this month, so here you go," I said, pulling out two stacks from my purse. "This should take care of everything for this month."

"Autumn Carrington, where did you get this money? I can't take this." She only called me by my government name when she was in serious mode.

"I've been saving up," I lied. If she knew how I'd gotten this money, I'm sure GiGi would have wasted no time whipping my twenty-nine year old ass and then she'd call the police to lock me up.

"Autumn, don't lie to me," Granny replied.

"I'm not! I worked some overtime hours last month that helped me a lot. I don't want you to have to worry about your bills while you are trying to get your health together. This is one less thing for you to concern yourself about, so please take it, Gi-Gi," I said.

"Sugar, this money better be clean. You know I don't take no blood money from the devil. Whatever I need, God will provide," GiGi said.

"GiGi, I wouldn't even come in here like that. I know you

would kick my behind," I said, avoiding eye contact with her. If she looked me in the eyes, she'd know I was lying.

"And don't you forget." She laughed. "You want something to eat? I got some collards, mac and cheese, and fried catfish in there."

"You know I'm not going to turn that down," I replied. I headed to GiGi's kitchen. The smell of the food hit my nostrils and my stomach responded with a growl. GiGi grabbed a plate from the cabinet and started loading it up.

"GiGi, you don't have fix my plate. I can do it. Have a seat, young lady," I playfully said.

"Sugar baby, I got this. I ain't handicapped."

"I know GiGi, but you should be getting your rest."

"Girl, hush! Anyway, how are you doing? Have you been taking care of yourself? And where is Lucky? I haven't seen him in a while now?" GiGi asked

"GiGi, I'm fine. And Lucky and I broke up a few months ago," I admitted. Tamela was the only other person who knew that Lucky and I were no longer a thing. GiGi looked at me with concern in her eyes.

"You sure you ok, baby? Those dark circles under your eyes got you looking really tired, again. You know what happens to you when you don't get enough rest."

"I promise I'm ok, GiGi. I'm going to try to catch up on some rest this weekend, but until then, I got a lot to do."

"Are you taking your meds?"

"GiGi, I don't mean any disrespect, but I don't want to keep talking about this. There is nothing wrong with me. I'm fine! I can promise you one thing, I'm not going to end up like

Winter if that's what you're worried about. I never want to be anything like her."

"Listen here, your mama had her struggles, but I ain't gonna let you sit and speak on her like that. You have no idea of all the things she went through. And I know you don't think so, but she loved you. She always wanted what was best for you. She just couldn't give it to you. I'll tell you one thing, if you're even close to having any issues again, you need to be honest with yourself about it. You're never going to have the life you desire living a lie and hiding from the truth!"

"I'm sorry, GiGi. You keep making excuses for my mother. What about my pain? You keep talking about how I have no idea what she went through. I do have an idea because I went through my own struggles. Sitting in a filthy apartment with no food to eat for days. Being beat because I reminded her of my father. What she did to me wasn't acceptable on any level. I'm sorry, GiGi, but it's just too hard," I said. Tears streamed down my face. GiGi hated whenever I had anything negative to say about Winter. Even though she was the source of a lot of pain for me, I never wanted to hurt GiGi.

"Don't be sorry. Just be compassionate. Have a little compassion towards your mother's situation. You never know when you might need that same level of compassion extended to you." GiGi placed the plate of food in front of me and sat down to watch me eat.

After spending the rest of the afternoon with GiGi, I headed home. Last night's events had me tired, and I needed to catch up on my sleep. I pulled up to the apartment complex and headed towards my building. I tugged at my coat as the chill in the air threatened to freeze my bones. I walked up the sidewalk when a handsome, tall stranger caught my eye. I blinked my eyes several times because I could have sworn it was Lucky. Of course, it couldn't have been him, though. Lucky was just a memory now, but resemblance to him was wild.

"That's the next one," Kalidah whispered to me.

"Why, though?" I inquired.

"You already know the count," she responded. "Go ahead and say something."

I obliged her and made my move.

Chapter Eighteen
Autumn

I studied the tall, caramel-complected man who stood about five feet in front of me. He was both familiar and a mystery, and I couldn't wait to get him back to his hotel room. I licked my lips as I thought about all of the things I wanted to do to him, but I tried to play it cool. Kalidah was itching to show herself. It had only been two days since we killed Lucky, but she was more than ready to take a life again.

"You ready?" He asked me as he ran his tongue across his thick lips. His saliva left a shine on them that made me want to suck them clean off his face.

"I been ready," I replied, wasting no time getting up from my seat at the bar. I grabbed my clutch and slid on my jacket. Alex grabbed me by my hands and led me to the door.

The coolness of the night nipped at my face, yet it sent a power surge through my body. I loved cool fall nights and the briskness in the air. I shivered a bit as a gust of wind threatened to snatch my honey blond curly wig from my head.

"You cold?" Lex asked.

"No. I'm good. This is actually my favorite kind of weather," I replied with a wide smile plastered on my face. Kalidah lurked within, watching the night unfold.

We headed across the street to the hotel. The street was eerily quiet. We passed by an old, homeless man sitting on a bench. I grabbed a hundred-dollar bill from my clutch and slid it in his cup. Lex followed suit and we rushed toward the hotel entrance. As the wind howled, I heard a voice whisper to me.

"A thousand good deeds cannot change the darkness of a tainted mind and heart."

"Excuse me, sir. What did you just say?" I asked. The man did not respond, he just threw up his hands.

"Did you hear him say something?" I asked Lex.

"Nah, I ain't hear shit but this wind," Lex responded as he pulled me in close and wrapped his arms around me.

"A thousand good deeds cannot change the darkness of a tainted mind and heart. When you accept who you are, then and only then will things change."

I heard the voice again but thought better of saying anything else about it. The last thing I wanted to do was ruin what was to come between Lex and me. I looked back at the homeless man sitting on the bench.

This time he looked up at me wearing a smile that displayed the four or five teeth he had in his head. It was clear that something or someone was trying to get my attention, but I wasn't sure who or what it was. Either way, I knew I'd never forget this night.

* * *

Lᴇx sᴛᴀʀᴇᴅ ɪɴᴛᴇɴᴛʟʏ ɪɴᴛᴏ Kᴀʟɪᴅᴀʜ's ᴇʏᴇ ᴀs sʜᴇ ʀᴏᴄᴋᴇᴅ her hips back and forth on his dick. For a second, I thought I was looking at her with Lucky because the resemblance was so striking. Although his face reminded me of Lucky's, his dick was anything but the quality that we were used to. But we weren't here to enjoy the moment. We were here to do two things. Satisfy our personal urges and help Ezrail satisfy his clients.

"Let me taste you," Lex whispered to Kalidah.

"You wanna taste me? How bad do you want it?" She asked as she leaned in to kiss his full lips. I watched the interaction with anticipation of our finishing act. At this moment, I was simply a voyeur.

"Bad. Real bad, ma."

"But, tonight isn't about me. It's about you and what you want."

"Well, I told you what I wanted, so why don't you let me serve you up?" Lex asked.

"Ok, I guess I can handle that request," Kalidah said.

I got up off of him so that he could get on top. As soon as I laid on my back, he hungrily spread my legs and went to work on devouring my pussy. He enjoyed it way more than we did. My mind was on how and when Kalidah was going to kill him. I knew why he had to die, and it was simply because when I saw him, he reminded me of the one who broke my heart. Kalidah hated any reminder of the pain that Lucky inflicted.

Lex finally came up for air. I watched as Kalidah took over and pretended his head game was some of the best she ever had. I could tell he really thought he had done something, but all that licking at our clit like it was a lollipop didn't do anything but make me mad. I didn't have the heart to tell him, but thought maybe Kalidah would be the one to let him know his bedroom game was trash. She didn't, though. It wouldn't matter after tonight, anyway.

"That was amazing!" Kalidah lied. "Now, I need you to hit this from the back." I got on my knees and I arched my wide ass in the air. Lex forcefully slid into my sweet spot. He was rough and aggressive with his stroke which caused my pussy to dry up.

The moonlight danced on the hotel wall, and I tried to focus on it, instead of this miserable experience. To speed up the process and help my juices flow, I rubbed my clit to get wet again.

"Get on top of me," Kalidah whispered as I pulled my ass away from him, disconnecting our bodies. I laid down and continued to massage my clit. Lex entered me again and began to ride me. I began to catch his movements and tighten the grip of my pussy on his dick. This started to drive him insane.

"You like that?" Kalidah asked.

"Yeah, I love it."

"You do? Tell me it's the best you've ever had," she commanded. Looking up at him, his eyes were closed and we both could tell he was closing in on his climax.

"This pussy is damn sure the best pussy I've had," he obliged.

"You know what I want you to do next?"

"Nah, baby? What you need me to do?"

"I need you to say my name while you up in this pussy," Kalidah said. Our eyes were still trained on him even though he was oblivious to our stare.

"Kalidah, baby. This pussy is so good, Kalidah!"

"Shhhh. Not so loud baby. I like it when you say my name softly. So this time, tell me how good my pussy is, but this time lower your voice," She instructed.

"Kalidah. Oh, shit. Kalidah, this pussy is so good. I'm about to cum in it." As soon as he said those words, I reached for the blade I'd hidden under the pillow. Kalidah took control again.

"Baby, open your eyes and look at me while you cum," she said. I wanted him to see her take his life. As soon as his eyes opened, a smile spread across my face. Kalidah pulled the knife from under the pillow and buried it in his neck. I quickly pulled the knife out and wiped it across the sheets. Crimson liquid splattered from his body spraying my face and everything in the nearby vicinity. Lex held his neck and toppled over on me. Pushing off of me, I quickly got up.

"That's what you get for hurting me, Lucky! I took your voice so you can no longer lie to me or hurt me with your words," Kalidah whispered in his ear.

The room was a mess. Kalidah's way of handling things was reckless and required a lot of cleanup for Ezrail and his crew. Eventually, we would need to find a way to do what was needed without all the blood and gore, even though there was a part of me that liked it. Kalidah loved it.

Kalidah grabbed the top sheet that was on the floor and handed it to me to wipe the blood from my face and body.

"Well, Ms. Girl, it's time for me to go," she said. Removing the wig from my head, I released my jet-black curls.

Retrieving my phone from my purse, I pulled out the burner cell phone Ezrail gave me and called the number pre-programmed in the phone.

"It's done," I said and quickly ended the call. Immediately, the door to the connecting suite opened and Kaylie, the woman I saw Ezrail meet a while ago, and Ezrail entered the room.

"Go ahead over there and get cleaned up. I left you some fresh clothes to put on and another wig," Ezrail said. "Your money is inside the nightstand drawer."

"Ok. Do you need me to help with anything else?" I asked.

"Nah, Ma. The only thing I need you to do is keep doing what you're doing. The more you embrace who you really are, the more you'll realize that what you thought was a curse is actually a gift. What the world sees as an illness, I see as a superpower. And you're the missing link that we needed to get shit done."

Chapter Nineteen
Autumn

Kalidah and I waited in the darkness of Whitney's Buckhead townhouse. I managed to swipe the keys to her place from Lucky on the night we killed him. I drove Lucky's car over there, so when she got home she'd think he was there waiting on her.

I walked through her home admiring how neat and clean she kept it. She was everything I wasn't and being in the space she shared with my fiancé made me realize exactly why Lucky chose her over me. And that shit crushed me.

There were pictures of Lucky and Whitney throughout her living room. What caught my eye was a glass heart figurine that had both Whitney and Lucky's picture etched within it. This would be perfect for what I needed it for.

"This nigga was really around here making another life with this bitch," Kalidah declared. "He played you, and that's exactly why the universe served him with the same energy he put out."

"I don't need you reminding me of the fact that I got played. I carry the pain from that with me everyday." The sound of Whitney's car entering the garage startled me. I hid in the powder room by the garage door entrance and waited for Whitney to enter.

"Baby, you home? Where you been?" Whitney called out as she entered the house through her garage. I held my breath as she walked past me.

"Bust that bitch in her head!" Kalidah yelled. Whitney, startled, turned around when she realized she wasn't in the house alone and it wasn't Lucky in her home. Before she could say a word, Kalidah took over and brought the glass heart crashing down into Whitney's forehead. She hit the floor with a thud and I rushed to grab her. We drug her body into her dining room and tied her up to a chair. Within about fifteen minutes, she regained consciousness.

"Where is Lucky, and why are you here?" she screamed.

Kalidah laughed. "We have unfinished business," Kalidah explained.

"And thanks to you, Lucky is dead," I added.

"Dead? What do you mean he's dead?" Confusion and fear spread across her face.

"I mean no longer living and currently taking a dirt nap like you'll soon be doing."

"Yep! You fucked with the wrong one this time," Kalidah interjected. She pushed the burgundy curls of the wig she was wearing out of her face.

"Bitch, why are you talking like that?" Whitney asked in response to the heavy sound of Kalidah's voice. She was used to hearing the sweet, childlike voice I had. Kalidah's voice boomed and was a few octaves lower than mine although it was still feminine.

"Oh, so you're feeling bold enough to be asking questions right now? If I were you, I'd shut the fuck up."

"You're a crazy ass bitch!" Whitney mumbled.

"We'll show you crazy." I pulled out the straight razor I kept in my boot and held it to her neck.

"Now what was that shit you were talking before?"

"I'm sorry, please don't hurt me." The sound of piss hitting the wood floor brought a look of embarrassment to Whitney's face.

"Aww somebody's scared now! I want you to beg for your life right now."

"I'm sorry, please don't kill me. Please don't kill me. Please. I won't tell anyone about tonight if you let me go," She pleaded.

"I want you to say, 'Please don't kill me, Kalidah' and I need you to say it in the softest voice you can find.

"Please don't kill me. Please don't kill me, Kalidah," she whispered. After she said the magic words, approached her from behind and grabbed her head. Whitney squirmed and tried to fight back, but she was no match for the adrenaline that coursed through my veins. Tired of playing games with her, Kalidah took control and slashed the dirty bitch's neck.

Like clockwork, Ezrail showed up. This was an unplanned kill, so Ezrail was actually helping me out by cleaning up my mess. He was still able to come up off this kill though, so he slid me a brown paper bag.

"Make sure y'all call me *before* you decide to kill so I can make sure we're good to go. We had other plans tonight, but I was able to shift some things around. Kaylie is going to run the clean up. I gotta head to the other side of town."

I simply nodded to acknowledge what Ezrail said. As I watched Kaylie and the others clean up Whitney's body and remove her organs, a feeling of sadness came over me. I didn't feel good about any of the shit I'd been doing. The darkness of my soul was taking over and that was too much for me.

"You don't look so well," Kaylie pointed out. "Listen, I know this work can be overwhelming. Take this," she said, handing two small baggies. One contained a white powdery substance, and the other contained four pills. "Pick your poison. Either way, it will help you take the edge off."

When I returned home, I sat in the darkness of my living crying. Between my bouts of tears, I was in the bathroom throwing up. Over the last couple of months, the nausea I was experiencing previously, intensified. I decided to take the other pregnancy test I had left from the box Tam brought me a few weeks ago.

I squatted to piss and passed the stick through my urine to catch the sample. After I was finished, I plopped down on the toilet and sat there. I reached down for jeans and pulled out the baggies Kaylie gave me and a lighter. I prepared the pack of heroin and filled the syringe that was in the pack with the substance. Before I could decide which one I wanted to try to numb my pain, the banging at my door interrupted me.

A familiar voice stood on the other side of my apartment door. It was my mother. How she knew where I lived was beyond me. Then again, I knew GiGi had probably given her my address at some point.

"Autumn! Autumn! Let me in! Please!" She sounded high and drunk and rather than allow her to continue to embarrass me by all the commotion she was causing, I opened my door to let her in.

"What the fuck are you doing here, Winter? And you had the nerve to show up here drunk and high!" I screamed.

"Watch who the fuck you talking to! I'm still your mother!" she asserted.

"You ain't my mother! You ain't never been a mother to me. GiGi is my mother. I just came out of your raggedy ass pussy!"

Wham! Winter forced her open palm into the side of my face.

"You gone learn to respect me! You little bitch! Standing there looking just like the nigga who left me to raise you alone."

"Bitch, you better not put your hands on Autumn again, or that'll be the last time you do it," Kalidah screamed.

Winter laughed, taking a seat on my couch. "Oh, so she's here now? You finally let your little friend out to play, I see." I ignored her comment.

"You on that shit again, I see. My daddy being out in them streets ain't have shit to do with me. Didn't you get enough of whooping my ass as a kid? Then you have the nerve to come over here fucked up!"

"You know what? You're just like me. As much as you want to be something different and as much as you want to have something different, you can't run away from the fact that you're just as fucked up in the head as I am. It's only a matter of time before you'll be looking for your fix to numb your pain."

Her words hit me like a ton of bricks considering the fact that I was just contemplating whether or not I wanted to swallow some pills or shoot up some drugs into my arm. Kalidah, sensing my pain, got up and went to the bathroom to retrieve the drugs I had. In the midst of all that I had going on, I'd recently contemplated taking a page out of my mother's playbook and tried curing my pain with drugs.

"You know what, Winter, since you love drugs so much, why don't you take this?" Kalidah teased. She held both the syringe and pills up in Winter's face. Winter swallowed hard. Beads of sweat formed at her hairline.

"Get the fuck out my face!" Winter screamed. "You don't know my life! You don't know what I've been through! You have no fucking idea how hard it is carrying this baggage I got. Then you want to sit here and play in my face, taunting me because you think this shit is cute!"

"You sure you don't want it?" Kalidah taunted. "I know you want it. You always wanted this more than you wanted anything else. You wanted it more than you wanted to be a mother, you trifling bitch, so I'm going to let you have exactly what you want." Without another word, Kalidah shoved the syringe of heroin into Winter's arm and pumped the contents into her veins.

The potency of the drugs in the syringe filled Winter's veins, causing her eyes to roll back in her head. Her mouth gaped, releasing saliva that traveled from her mouth, down her chin, and onto her shirt.

"Mommy! Mommy! Get up!" I screamed. "Kalidah! What did you do? What did you do?" I paced the floor trying to figure out what my next move was while winter's body convulsed.

Who to call? If I should call the police or ambulance. I checked Winter's pulse and it was fading fast. I grabbed her in my arms and rocked gently back and forth. I thought of calling Ezrail but decided to hit Tam up instead. I needed her in this moment.

"Tam! Please help me! Please help me! I killed my mama! I mean, Kalidah killed my mama! Winter is gone die. I can't do this anymore! I can't do this! I wanna die, too!" I was so out of it that I don't even know what Tam said to me.

Less than ten minutes later, Tam entered my apartment to find me holding my mother in my arms and crying. That was the last thing I remembered.

Chapter Twenty
Autumn

The room was cold and gray. With my knees pulled into my chest, I rocked back and forth on the tiny bed to stay warm. I could hear and see people moving about on the other side of the window in the door. Keys jingled at the door, which soon opened.

Dr. Michaels appeared in his traditional white coat and black rimmed glasses. He looked and me then paused to make a few notes on his iPad. Pulling out the chair that was tucked under the small metal table in the corner of the room, he sat down.

"Ms. Carrington, how are you feeling today?" he asked as he leered at me from above his glasses. A piece of his dark brown hair fell from out of place and tickled his eyebrow. He pushed it back in place and continued to stare.

I sucked in the cool air of the room and exhaled. My patience was running thin, and so was Kalidah's. "Let us the fuck out of here!" I growled. "I've got shit to do."

"Hmph. I see. And just who do you mean by 'we?'"

A smile spread across my face. Dr. Michaels knew exactly who I was referring to. Kalidah and I absolutely hated how he tried to patronize us. It would only be a few more minutes before Kalidah would speak up for herself. "Why we gotta play games? You already know who I'm referring to."

"Which voice are you hearing today? It seems others have manifested since you've been here."

"Dr. Michaels, don't be an asshole. You know I am the dominant one here. Like you said, the others are new. However, I have and will always run this shit," Kalidah asserted.

"Exactly, Doc, you already know Kalidah is now with me every day. Ezrail helped me to embrace her. He told me she helps to give me courage to do the things I want to do. She helps do the things I was scared of being judged for doing. She's protected me my whole life and today is not different."

"What things are those, Ms. Carrington? And who is this Ezrail person?"

"You know already. Why do you continue to ask me questions you already know the answer to?"

"So Kalidah gives you courage to kill others?"

"Kill others? Is that what you think this has been about? She protects me. I don't kill anyone. I could never take a life. It's Kalidah. The blood will always be on her hands. Ezrail's too."

"How many people have you killed, Ms. Carrington?"

"Didn't you hear a thing I just said? You can't be as stupid as you look. I'm not going to continue repeating myself. I didn't kill anyone! When am I getting out, Doc?"

"Ms. Carrington, I'm afraid I can't answer that question.

It's clear you're not well. You've been hallucinating and now you seem to think you— I mean Kalidah has killed people. Your whole family is concerned about you. Your grandmother thinks you need to stay here a bit longer."

"The one person who cared about me is sick and dwindling away while I'm in here." My voice softened at the thought of GiGi and the pain I know I've caused her over the last couple of years. The shame and embarrassment I brought her made me feel some kind of way. Hurting her is the only thing I've regretted the most. I had no regret for nothing else. I did what I had to do. But, GiGi never deserved to have her heart broken by me. She gave me everything she had to make sure I turned into a decent person.

A tear fell down my face, hitting the blue hospital gown that adorned my body. Quickly wiping the tear away, I looked up to see that Ezrail had entered the room. Although he was silent, I could hear his voice in my ear.

"Never give them your tears unless it's needed to accomplish the mission. Tears with no purpose only exploit your weaknesses."

"I know. I'm sorry," I whispered.

"Autumn, who are you talking to? What are you sorry about?" Dr. Michaels asked.

"I'm sorry that I'm stuck here and not able to do the work I need to do." My gaze stayed trained on the corner where Ezrail stood. He watched my interaction with Dr. Michaels carefully.

Dr. Michaels continued to scribble in his notepad. Deep down inside, I wanted to grab his pen and ram into his throat. That would be a rookie move, though. I'm sure he expected me to do something like that given the fact that two guards stood outside the door peering into the room periodically to make sure I was on my best behavior.

"Sweet Autumn, you still have time to turn this around. Remember what I told you. The Highest One is still waiting for you. You are still treasure, Autumn. Your life still has meaning, and He's the one that can change all of this for you. The choice will always be yours."

Alya sat next to me on the cold, hard bed but she brought warmth with her that temporarily covered my body. A calmness and sense of peace came over me, but the fullness in my heart began to betray me as the tears started to fill the wells of my eyes again. There were too many for me to hold back, so they spilled over soaking my shirt. I was overwhelmed at the thought of anyone thinking I was still treasure. So overwhelmed that I couldn't find the words to speak to Alya.

Ezrail left his corner to approach Alya. His menacing physique towered over Alya's, but she didn't let that intimidate her. What I admired about her was that she held her own with him. She did most things with grace, but Alya knew how to get down and dirty when she needed to. I had a feeling that this was a moment that she was willing to show her other side.

"Don't you think it's a bit too late for you to be trying to get her?" Ezrail asked Alya.

"You should know as well I do that it's never too late for me. The Most High gives everyone a chance until they take their last breath. That's the only time it will be too late. Considering the fact that Autumn is still alive and breathing, she's still a viable candidate for a team switch," Alya assured.

"She's too far gone. She'll never switch up. I gave her access to things that she wanted and I did it quickly. We both know

that the Most High tends to take his time with giving people their deepest desires. We're prepared to shift this situation for Autumn, too. She knows what she has to do."

"What she's been required to do is the reason why she's here. Perhaps your way isn't the way she needs," Alya maintained.

"Both of y'all just need to shut the hell up!" I yelled. I jumped up off the bed, agitated and enraged!

"Ms. Carrington, have a seat!" Dr. Michaels demanded.

"What the fuck are you going to do if she doesn't? You don't scare me. I've killed men twice your size. Killing you wouldn't be that fucking hard to do," Kalidah said.

"Guard! Guard!" Dr. Michaels yelled to alert the guards to come in. At that moment, I ran up on Dr. Michaels and tried to get the pen out of his hand. The guard opened the door, and two large male medical assistants charged me, restrained me, and injected me with something that made me tired. The last thing I remember seeing was Ezrail and Alya as they stood in the corner watching silently as I lost the rest of what was left of my mind.

I AWOKE WITH A THROBBING HEADACHE. THE SUNLIGHT danced off the wall and caused me to wince at the brightness it brought into the room. I looked around the room I was in. It was drastically different from the room I was in with the padded walls and steel door. Realizing I was in a hospital room, I immediately tried to get out the bed, but realized I was strapped down. Immediately I started to panic. Relief washed over me as I realized my grandmother was sitting next to me on the bed.

"Sugar Baby, how you feeling? You look a lot better. You've been out of it for a while now." GiGi got up from her seat at the side of my bed and leaned down to kiss my forehead.

"I'm ok, GiGi. What are you doing here?" I questioned. "I thought you were in the hospital sick. You look fine to me."

"Sugar, what are you talking about? I am fine."

"What about the cancer?"

"Well, I'll just have to see what the doctor says in a month or so. I'm kicking cancer's butt. It ain't gonna kick mine! Didn't I tell you that the good Lord has been taking good care of me."

"GiGi, who's been taking you to your treatments since I've been here? Have you had enough money for your bills? I need to get out of here."

"Relax, Sugar baby. Everything has been fine. You don't need to be worried about me. You need to be focusing on that baby you've been carrying that will be here soon."

"Baby? What baby? How did I even end up here? Dr. Michaels said Winter is the reason I'm here."

"I don't know how to tell you this, but, Autumn, Winter is dead. She relapsed and overdosed on Fentanyl. She died at your house. You don't remember? My baby's been gone for about three months now. I guess you tried to push that memory out of your brain just like all the others." Tears filled GiGi's eyes.

"No, GiGi, that's not true. I saw Winter. I saw her. I saw her not that long ago, and she was fine."

"Baby, I don't think you're feeling well. If you think you saw your mother, you're seeing things. As much as I hate to admit it, she's gone. My poor Sugar Baby. Them demons done got a hold of ya, and they ain't trying to let you go." As a tear streamed down GiGi's face, I could see the anguish in her eyes.

"I'm sorry, GiGi. I know what I saw, and I'm not crazy. I'm just fine and normal. I'm not like Winter! I don't want to be like Winter."

"Autumn, you can't hide from who you are, but the good thing is that God is always ready to help you when you surrender those things that you can't change to him. You see, baby, you can't get over this by yourself. Only God can help you. You just have to ask. I done prayed and prayed, baby. The word says that where two or three are gathered in His name, He is there in the midst. Sugar baby, I need you to pray with me for your healing."

Tears formed in my eyes. I couldn't believe all that I'd put my GiGi through. She grabbed my hands and gently kissed me on the cheek.

"Where is Lucky? Doesn't he know I'm going to have his baby? Doesn't he know I'm in here? He should be with me right now." I tried to get up from the bed but realized I was restrained to it.

"Baby, Lucky is dead. He was murdered. They found him hacked up in his apartment. All his organs were missing."

"Murdered. Mmmmm-murdered. GiGi, you mean he's dead?"

"I'm afraid so, baby." Flashes of the night I killed Lucky ran through my mind. I didn't want to believe I had done such a thing to the man I loved. Here I was, pregnant with his child. The one thing I always wanted other than being his wife. The tears started again. I thought about what GiGi had just said to me. I was ready to be honest with myself about who I was and the state of my mind for the sake of my child.

"Pray with me, GiGi," I softly said.

"Of course, baby. But I got somebody else I think could help us with this prayer. I asked one of the hospital Chaplains to come by here. Let me see if she is outside." GiGi kissed my face once again before peeking her head outside of my room.

"She's ready, Chaplain," GiGi said.

At that moment, a woman bearing a close resemblance to Alya – wearing a black dress with a clergy collar, a cross necklace, diamond stud earrings, and carrying a leather Bible – entered my room. "Hello, Autumn, it's a pleasure to see you. Your grandmother told me what's going on with you."

"Thank you. Nice to see you as well," I said.

"Chaplain Thomas, thank you so much for coming here to pray with us," GiGi said.

"No problem. Let's get to it. Let's take hands." Alya walked to the other side of my bed. She grabbed one hand and GiGi grabbed the other. "Lord, we thank you for this day. We thank you for being a God of second chances. We thank you for keeping Autumn in the midst of her indiscretions. We thank you for the life that is now growing inside of her. Lord, we ask that you renew Autumn's mind. Give her the serenity to accept the things she cannot change, the courage to change the things she can, and the wisdom to know the difference. Lord, let her give you the things she cannot change on her own. We know that with you, though, it's possible for the change to happen. Lord, we cancel the attack of the enemy against her mind and her life. We cancel the attack of the assignment of the enemy on her unborn child's life. Even though the enemy may have believed he had her for keeps, we know that you are a vindicating God. Right now, you are vindicating Autumn. Lord, we seal this prayer. It is so, and so it is."

"Thank you, Chaplain Thomas," I said softly. I wanted to believe in the power of that prayer. I wanted to believe that finally God would hear me and not just allow me to live off my GiGi's prayers. I needed my prayers to touch Heaven, too.

"Autumn, God hears you. Don't ever think that he doesn't. He will always be here for you. He can change your situation in the blink of an eye. One day you will realize he's done just that," Alya said. Leaving me with those words, she left the room.

"Baby, do you feel any better?" GiGi asked.

"Somewhat, GiGi. How can you be here with me after all the bad things that I've done? I've let you down. I've killed people. Kalidah, the voice in my head told me to do a lot of ugly things."

"Baby, what are you talking about? I think you need to get some rest. You're gonna need your strength to bring that precious baby into the world in a few days."

I stared out the window. It seemed like GiGi was under the impression that all the bad things I'd done didn't happen, but I was under the impression that they did. Seeing Alya today was proof of that. She was real, so all the things that happened to me over the nine months had to be, too.

"Baby, GiGi has gotta get home now, but I will be up here in the morning. I gotta get some rest if I'm going to be ready to see my baby have my baby. Oh, and your daddy is home. He'll be here, too."

"What? When did he get home?" I asked, puzzled at the mention of my father.

"He got home 3 months ago. He had to spend that time in a halfway house, but now he's being released."

"That's good to hear. Well, I'll see you tomorrow GiGi."

"Okay, baby. Get some rest. The new dose of medication you're on has been making you pretty tired anyway. Love you, Sugar Baby.

"Love you, too." GiGi walked out of my room and went on her way. I lay there with tears in my eyes. With my one free hand, I rubbed my stomach. My baby moved around letting me know he or she was alive and well.

"I can't believe I am having a baby," I whispered to myself. I thought about the events of the last few months and couldn't believe that I was locked up in the hospital right now. The only reason why I probably wasn't on the psych floor was because of the baby I was carrying.

"Yeah, bitch, be thankful you're in here now. You acted a damn fool up there the other night. Ezrail got more work for us to do, but our baby is about to be in our way. Don't think because you had that little prayer session that I am going back into hiding."

"Shut up! Shut up! Shut up! I hate you! I hate you! I hate you!" I yelled out. I was tired of the voices in my head tormenting me.

Two Months Later...
Autumn

I slept horribly last night. Kalidah and the new voices that were in my head decided they wanted to show up and fight to stay in control of me. I went through a range of emotions all night long. The broken little girl who showed up cried off and on, wondering where her mother was. Kalidah raged with anger as the other voices were too scrambled for me to understand. I was exhausted, and there was no medicine I could be given. So, I eventually wore myself out enough to get a little rest.

My doctor had been in about four hours ago to start the labor induction process. The doctors decided it would be best to go ahead and deliver the baby now so that I could get the mental health treatment I needed to receive. There were effective medications that I needed to take but couldn't do so while I was pregnant.

"Sugar baby! Hey! Hey! Guess who I have with me?" GiGi

entered my room loud and boisterous. Aunty Tweety and my father trailed behind her.

"Hey, niecey pooh! How you feeling?" Aunt Tweety asked.

"Just tired and in a lot of pain," I complained. My father walked over to my bed, stroked my hair, and kissed me on my forehead.

"Hey baby girl," he said. My tears choked me. I couldn't find the words to express how I was feeling at that moment. I'd only seen my daddy wearing a jumpsuit and behind a glass window. To see him standing there was overwhelming.

"Daddy, I can't believe you're here. I'm so happy to see you." My heart was full.

"Thanks baby girl, I'm home now and I ain't going nowhere again. I want to be here for you and my grandbaby."

My nurse came into my room to check to see if I was ready to push my baby out. After checking me, she called the doctor in.

"Ms. Carrington, it looks like you're ready to push this baby out. Do you want everyone in here for the delivery?"

"Yes, I'd like my family to be here." GiGi pushed her chair beside my bed and held my hand as we started the delivery process. Twelve pushes later, and my daughter took her first breath. Deep down I was hoping for a boy. I didn't want a girl to continue the curse that was on me and my mother.

"Oh my goodness! She look just like you and your mother," GiGi squealed with excitement. The doctor handed me my baby and tears immediately filled my eyes. She had Lucky's nose and eyes, but the she had my lips and face shape. She was beautiful. My heart was sad that Lucky wasn't here and we couldn't be the family I alway dreamed we could be.

"Wow! I got a grandbaby!" my daddy exclaimed. "I'm gonna have to keep my gun loaded to keep the suckers away from her."

"What you gone name her?" Aunt Tweety asked.

"Well, I was thinking of naming her Summer. Summer Roberta Carrington."

"That's beautiful! I'm honored that you gave my great grandbaby my name! I can't wait to get her home so we can spoil her. I'm going to take good care of her while you're here. She won't be going into the system."

"GiGi, I want to take care of my own baby."

"I know, Sugar Baby, and you will be able to once you get your mental health together first."

*　*　*

GIGI, AUNT TWEETY, AND MY DADDY LEFT THE HOSPITAL for the day, but assured me they'd be back the next morning. I lay in my bed staring at the crib next to me. I couldn't believe I was finally a mother. Being a single mother was never part of the plan.

A light tap at the door interrupted my thought. I looked up to see Ezrail dressed in scrubs and pushing a cart that contained what was supposed to be my dinner.

"What are you doing here?" I asked.

"I wanted to check in on you. And I didn't want you to think that you having a baby changes anything with our agreement. Whenever you're healed, I need you and Kalidah back on the team to help."

"Nah, I can't do it. Things are different now. I'm a mom. Besides, I haven't heard from Kalidah in months."

Ezrail walked over to the crib and peeped at Summer. "She's beautiful just like you. I can already tell that she's going to be special just like you were."

"What do you mean special just like I *was*?" I inquired knowing full well what he meant.

"The voices will find her, too. And when they do, I wonder how she'll respond?"

"Nah, she ain't going to hear no voices."

"That's what you think. You might as well embrace her destiny." Ezrail looked from me to my baby then abruptly left us alone in the room. I scooped my baby up in my arms and studied her face. She was beautiful. All I could see was Lucky's face when I looked at her. It was a reminder of the dream I had that would never be a reality. Tears came from out of nowhere and blinded me. Summer deserved a family with a mother and a father, but she'd never have that. And Ezrail suggesting that she'd have the same mental struggles I had saddened me even more.

"Autumn. Let me out. Let me see our baby," Kalidah's voice whispered to me.

"Leave me alone!" I yelled. Placing Summer back in her crib, I got up and took a pillow off my bed. I kissed my sweet baby's cheek and placed the pillow over her head. Her little feet flapped as she struggled for air, but I held the pillow in place until she stopped moving.

I sent a text to GiGi and my father letting them know I was sorry and that I couldn't bear the thought of my daughter struggling like I did. Once the text was sent, I took a sheet from my bed and went into the bathroom. Standing on the bench in the shower, I tightly wound the sheet around my neck and then tied it to the shower rod. I stood there for a minute asking God for forgiveness for all of the bad things I'd done. Remorse hit me when I thought about the fact that I killed my baby.

"Lord, if you never answer another prayer, please hear this one. Please let my baby live. She deserves a chance and I didn't mean to hurt her." I let the remaining tears fall and made peace with my decision to end my life.

"Autumn," Kalidah's voice whispered to me for the last time
Ignoring Kalidah's voice, I kicked the bench from under me. I struggled to breathe, but death was quickly approaching to claim me. As I took my last breath, I heard my baby gasp followed by her cries filling the room. My attempt to save her from the painful life I experienced failed. And that became the first time I realized God heard me and the only time I was thankful for being failure.

THE END

Acknowledgments

So, I finally did something I dreamed of doing, but I couldn't have done it without God first. He planted the seeds and sent many people along the way to water them. For that I am super thankful.

To my mom: Thank you for always staying on me. Thank you for pushing me to push past how I feel. Most importantly, thank you for praying for me. You know every facet of me and yet, your love for me has been unwavering. I love you so much!

To my daughters: My My and Li Li, thank you for being understanding most of the time when I said I needed to write and work on my books. I know there were many times that you wanted to do something or go somewhere, but you knew I was working. Thank you for your sacrifice. I love you both to infinity and beyond.

To My BFFS: Andrea and Brena! What can I say? We've been ten toes down for almost 30 years now. Nothing can change my love for you both. We may not always agree, but y'all better remember that y'all are stuck with me for life! I love you both!

To my coach T. Styles and the VP C. Wash: I never knew that when I met you both over ten years ago, you both would take up so much space in my heart! I love you both so very much. You both have such big hearts and I appreciate all of the love, support, and grace you have given me. Thank you for believing in me when you cast me as the Head Pitbull in Charge, Yvette. Thank you for believing in me now!

To The Prolific Pens (K Sherrie, Tina Marie, Kayne Doe, Amber Ghe, and M.K.Strong) : My love for each of you is immeasurable. You became my tribe and a source of inspiration and encouragement. It was an honor to pen The Sins of O.G. with you all. You all will forever have a special place in my heart! Let's pen another hit! We have some unfinished business to handle!

To Allison Grace: Thank you for being so supportive, believing in me, and giving me the amazing opportunity to be a Columnist for Intellectual Ink Magazine. You are a beautiful soul and have been an amazing sister/friend. I love you!

To all of the Authors, Editors, Urban Lit Industry Influencers that I have met over the years who have been kind and supportive (Kimani Lauren, Delia Rouse, Allor Henrique, Danni Terrell, Qwan Parker, Mz. Toni, Diane Rembert and many more) Thank you for embracing me. Thanks for the kind words. I love you all. Thank you all for the inspiration.

To my family, friends, former co-workers: Thank you for all the love and support. It does not go unnoticed. It means the world to me!

With Love,
    Shonda

About the Author

Shonda Mayes was born and raised in the Hampton Roads/757 area of Virginia. Considered a "Jackie of all Trades," Shonda has many talents. Shonda is the CEO and Founder of Grit, Grind, and Grace Publications. Gifted in writing and public speaking, Shonda decided to answer the call on her life and use her experiences to help other people. She's down-to-earth-and relatable due to the many life experiences that have molded her into the woman she is today. Her authenticity and transparency has allowed her to connect with others on a different level. Shonda also has a huge love for acting and was cast as Yvette from the popular "Pitbulls in a Skirt" book series by Mikal Malone. This was her first major acting role and she fell in love with the art of bringing characters to life. Shonda hopes to further pursue her dreams of acting.

Shonda currently resides in the Atlanta metro area with her two beautiful daughters. She hosts her own podcast, Just Shonda, where she and her guests discuss real life issues. She currently has several writing projects she is working on slated to be released 2022.

* * *

Let's stay in touch!

Join my email list to stay up to date on new releases, contests, prizes, and more! Head to my website to subscribe: www.shondamayes.com